The Whitby Horror
and other tales

By

Eddie Skelson

Pandemic Press

The Whitby Horror
and other tales

Contents

Foreword

Afterword

Foreword

Most of the stories in this collection are in some way connected to my Crowley series and novel Winter Falls. I think it's fine not to have read them, the tales should stand up on their own, but a reader who is unfamiliar with the world in which they are set, or explored in the offerings already mentioned, might feel a little adrift.

Exceptions to this are Two Doors Up which is a bit of Flash Fiction, and Fort Hope. Both were written with no thought of my world of the Aether and Essence and of course the Shadow and Void, but they could still be a part of it, if you really wanted them to. I included them because I liked them, and as I'm not likely to produce another collection for quite a while I thought why not give them a moment in the sun, or the darkness...

I hope you enjoy the book, thanks so much for giving my tales a shot. You can expect to see some of the characters again, and some you definitely won't.

Eddie Skelson Dec 2015

For John Stockton, who said I was a worthy pupil.

You sir, were a fantastic teacher.

THE WHITBY HORROR

The Daily Sport was Albert English's guilty secret. It was delivered to his home every day, but an arrangement with his newsagent ensured that it was tucked away inside a copy of The Times which was a far more reputable newspaper for the little piece of Whitby he called home.

Albert never read The Times. He found it immensely boring. Page after page of political mediocrity and financial speculation, and he still harboured bad memories of the immense broadsheet it had once been. At that time it had been almost impossible to read the damn thing outdoors and required Origami skills to fold it into a manageable size. However, even though they had finally given in and caught up to the 21st Century, the publishers of The Times still failed to fill it with anything that was of interest to him.

The Daily Sport on the other hand was fun. It was bright and fresh and always silly. The pages were often draped with alluring photographs of beautiful young ladies that made the ludicrous stories even more appealing, and although he had no interest in the ladies *per se* they added to the colour and sheer sauciness of the whole thing.

He loved the fantastic headlines and silly articles, 'World War Two Bomber Found on Moon,' and '2-Headed Santa Eats His Reindeer.' The shameless rag was filled scandals of A-list Celebrities who had been caught in *flagrante delicto* with each other and Albert relished the lurid revelations, even though he rarely knew who they were or what they might be famous for.

It was trivial and it was more often than not appallingly crass, but at ninety years old Albert felt that he should be allowed to get his fun wherever he could find it.

Today's Daily Sport headline was not so much fun, at least not for him. While the Times reported, 'Millions Are Being

Squandered Over Red Tape,' the Sport led with something entirely different and for Albert, far more worrying.

'Grisly Find on Whitby Beach!'

The headline screamed it out, as though it was pitching a Hammer House movie. Albert scanned the article quickly but still took in every word. Each poorly constructed sentence and entirely superfluous exclamation mark was committed to memory. What it told him was simple enough to take in but equally dreadful in prospect. He knew well enough when something was portentous and this was an all singing, all dancing portent of extreme nature.

After the past week's storms across the north-east, culminating in a terrific downpour two nights ago, parts of the cliff that faced the famous Whitby coast had fallen into the sea overnight. What every local, and every gothic horror fan knew, was that situated atop this cliff was the equally famous churchyard featured in Bram Stokers horror classic, Dracula.

Thanks almost wholly to this connection Whitby had become a Mecca for fans of horror movies of the eighties, and an annual meeting place for Goths. Albert didn't quite understand Goths, but then he didn't understand experimental Jazz either and so let the two matters of taste lie under 'things best left alone' in his vast repository of life experiences.

The extent of the erosion was made clear as rotting coffins and skeletal remains could be seen protruding from the freshly exposed cliff face. Further to this, a human skull had washed up onto the nearby shore causing great alarm in residents. It was all quite ghastly, quite lurid and The Sport had really gone to town on the piece because of this.

As well as a headline shouting out from the front page there was a grainy photograph of the church and its rows of ageing headstones. Even in the centre pages the story took up the whole upper portion, with more photographs of the church, the abbey and the storm beaten cliff. The bottom section was filled with bullet-pointed facts concerning Bram Stoker and his use of the abbey as the setting for Dracula. There was also a small editorial on the Goth's and horror fans, who were drawn to the site because of its fictional history.

With typical Daily Sport flair, a topless model had been edited into the frame of the abbey. They had painted her up to look vaguely like a Goth, although she actually looked as though a band member from Kiss had undergone a gender transition. She was about to kiss, with heavily lipstick coated crimson lips, a grinning and patently plastic skull.

'Oh dear,' Albert said.

The phone rang. It was loud and shrill and gave him a start. It sat on a small coffee table next to the leather armchair in which he always read his papers. Albert took a breath and picked up the receiver.

Before he could offer a polite 'hello' the schoolmasterly voice of Norris Garvey barged down the line.

'Have you seen the damned papers?' Norris demanded.

He was the oldest of their group and surely the biggest pain in the backside. Grumpy, cynical, breathtakingly arrogant and severely quick tempered.

'I've just this minute read it Norris,' Albert replied, his voice a mousey whisper compared to the boom of his friend.

'We need to meet up, and fast.'

'I suppose we should,' Albert agreed. 'Do you think that Alf will have seen it?'

'Don't be ridiculous,' Norris barked. 'Alfred will be pissing about in his allotment. He never reads the bloody papers until gone noon.'

'Ah, yes,' Albert replied almost apologetically.

Albert felt that he should defend his friend but Norris was clearly perturbed and it was best not to engage him in any form of argument or discussion when his back was up. It wasn't worth the hours of ranting and moaning about 'the state we are in' or 'things have gone bum-tiddly since we let 'insert his current pet peeve here' ruin everything. And what was *bum-tiddly*? Albert had no clue or desire to question Norris's bizarre little descriptions.

Albert thought Norris was being unfair on Alf, he *did* read the papers as he was required too, just not in the morning. Alf liked to be up early so he could potter around amongst his vegetables rather than sit waiting for the daily waffle to arrive and trudge through it all looking for anything odd. Even Albert had grown bored of it after all these years, he wondered if perhaps it was a sign that it was time to move on, to let some new blood take over. He had begun to earnestly wish it was so.

'We'll meet down there, at the allotment. I suggest we try to convene no later than…,' there was a pause.

Albert visualised Norris staring at his watch and waiting for the minute hand to hit a solid number, '…let's say ten.'

Albert looked at the silver clock sitting on top of his fireplace, it was 09.50 to the second.

'We can check out the scene and have a cup of tea at Giuseppe's afterwards,' Norris added in a less terse tone

'Right oh,' Albert replied.

The receiver went dead and he returned it to its cradle. Tea would be nice. If the world was in danger of being completely destroyed it was best to approach the situation with a good hot cup of fine Yorkshire blend.

***

Giuseppe's Tea Room was small and deliberately unappealing. Named after its owner, a small, restless import from Sicily, the cafe was the haunt of Whitby locals and the 'tourist unfriendly' attitude of Giuseppe sat well with many of them.

In December, in fact all through the winter Whitby became the stereotypical northern town that Morrissey might approve of. Colourful hanging baskets and fluorescent A-boards were packed away and dubious street vendors went into hibernation. Grey skies diluted the formerly verdant green of surrounding hills and the seemingly endless rain washed away the colour of the place. But as many businesses' pulled down their shutters, and their proprietors prayed for an early spring, Giuseppe's Tea Room continued to service its regular crowd, tourists be damned.

The three friends entered the Tea Room. Norris strode in first. He was tall at six feet but liked to point out whenever he could that he had been six foot two in his prime. He tapped the floor with his beautifully crafted, polished oak cane. Many tall men found in later years, even if they had not suffered injuries to their legs or back in younger days, that they had begun to stiffen a little, but not Norris.

Like Albert and Alfred, he had never had an ache, or pain or cold or any form of natural illness since he was eighteen. He simply liked the look that tall men with canes presented and above all of this it seemed proper. He was slim and this befitted his height but he wasn't at all skinny, he had kept the athletic build he had acquired during his army days, but this had to be hidden.

At five foot six Albert was the shortest of the trio. He carried a little weight around his waist and also in his tidily moustached face but was by no means fat, '*comfortably sized*,' he usually remarked. He had served his war time deep underground plotting and reporting the movement of troops, advising those who lead the war against the Nazi's as best he could to prevent harm to the troops that he controlled with little pins on a vast board. For many years he had been a voice that Winston Churchill welcomed when down in the labyrinthine bunker of mission control.

Alfred, he preferred Alf, and only Norris called him Alfred but then he called everyone by their first name whether they liked it or not, was a little shorter than Norris but had the sturdiest build of the three. He was broad shouldered and had strong square hands. He was meticulously clean shaven and proud of his neatly cut, straight black hair that still only had the faintest lines of grey at the sides. What he had done during the war he had never told to a soul, not even to Norris and Albert although they were well aware of the unit in which he had fought. It was a secret even now and neither of his friends ever felt the need to press him for stories.

While Alfred had the hair of man in his thirties Norris's was a subtle mix of grey and white, short back and sides in traditional military style, whereas Albert had an untidy mess of wavy white locks. He resembled a chubby Einstein and always wore a colourful bow-tie and a bland beige zip-up jacket that could blend in with almost any surroundings while remaining perpetually out of fashion.

Anyone who saw the three friends for the first time might think that they were far younger than their years allowed. If birth certificates were to be believed Norris was the eldest at ninety-one and both Albert and Alfred were ninety. Nonagenarians, even the plucky, robust people who seemed to radiate life and vigour could not hold a candle to Norris, Alf and Albert as they strolled through the town. They walked into the Tea Room confidently and with backs straight, showing none of the stoop that most of the very elderly couldn't avoid.

As they entered, Giuseppe was wiping down the vinyl red and white checked tablecloth at their usual spot.

'Ahh!' he called out and made an exaggerated welcome gesture with arms his outstretched.

'The Three Musketeers are return!'

His accent was thick and his English occasionally broken. He pronounced Musketeers as Mooseketeers. Norris flinched a little.

'Are we alright for our usual table Giuseppe?' Albert enquired.

'Sure, sure. I just now finish it. You can sit.' Giuseppe pulled back a chair from the table.

The friends each took the space they occupied on every visit, Alf nearest the wall with Albert next to him, Norris sat opposite Albert.

Giuseppe took orders for three mugs of tea. When he returned and the beverages were distributed with thanks from each of the gents Giuseppe leaned in a little and lowered his voice.

'Eh... you seen the bloody newspapers right?' He pronounced bloody as 'bladdy,' but Norris let this slide too.

The gents looked at each other warily then nodded slowly.

'All bloody morning they been here you know?'

He crooked his head back a little to indicate a table in the far corner of the Tea Room where four men of varied age, all wearing donkey jackets sat with the remains of a fried breakfast in front of them.

'Bloody councilmen or something,' Giuseppe said, as though he had a table of Nazi's sat eating fried toast.

He leaned in a little closer and dropped his voice even lower. 'I charge em all a quid an extra for breakfast,' he winked, and wandered back to the counter at the back of the Tea Room where he liked to stand glowering at unfamiliar faces.

'Councilmen!' Albert echoed in an excited whisper once Giuseppe was out of earshot. 'Do you think that will cause problems?'

'No, I shouldn't think so,' Norris replied, 'they'll just be around to make sure there are no health and safety issues.'

'It's a cliff that's falling into the sea Noz,' Alf said, 'of course there are health and safety issues. Can you imagine the hullaballoo when some old dears Yorkshire Terrier gets flattened by a falling tombstone?'

Alf was never afraid to dig into Norris when he was being surly, obnoxious or just plain moody. He was, as far as the term could be applied to a pensioner, the tough guy of the group. Not brash or bullish but reserved and usually quiet, yet he refused to be brow-beaten or cowed with Norris's or anyone else's bluster.

Alf had boxed regularly into his late sixties but had stopped when people started to notice that he was strikingly fit and agile for a man who was well into drawing his pension. He didn't like or need the attention. None of them did.

Albert admired Alf immensely and in his deepest and most private thoughts he understood that he had always liked him much more than as a friend. His homosexuality had, by necessity in his past, been kept locked away under half a century of repression and suspicion by society. As a pleasant and exceptionally caring man, he had been delighted to see the gradual erosion of the barrier of misunderstanding that had prevented generally good people from seeing that gay people, he loved that term, were also just like everyone else.

Whenever Alf rounded on Norris a little shiver of glee ran through Albert's body. Yet he also admired Norris, or Nozzer as he and Alf called him. For certain he was an argumentative and somewhat blunt man, but over the years Noz had never failed to support his friends and had never let anyone gain the upper hand over him, and Albert was well aware that he was prone to only see the good in people. If it wasn't for Norris, Albert was sure that he would have bought a hundred timeshares and had his drive re-surfaced a dozen times.

'OK,' Norris said to move quickly on, 'we need a plan.'

Albert and Alf nodded in agreement.

'So what do we know?' Norris turned to Albert.

Albert clasped his fingers on the table. 'Well, the abbey has always been something of a magnet for... people who are interested in the supernatural, and it has always been the abbey that gets the most attention. Of course *we* all know that the Abbey is about as paranormally active as a Cornish pasty, however the churchyard is a different story.'

11

Albert looked about the cafe to ensure that there was no one listening in. Alf and Norris also took a sly look around.

'I did a little checking and there is something buried up there that might be a problem. Unfortunately, I don't know what it is, what it does or if there is any immediate threat to us, but all of my sources indicate a relic of some considerable power.'

'Do we know who put it there?' Alf said.

'We do,' Albert replied, 'it was Aleister Crowley.'

Norris rolled his eyes, 'I might have known.'

'Yes, it seems that he had it placed into a crypt which was then covered over. It must be quite deep if there are graves above it.'

'But we don't know why he did it, why he put it there?' Alf asked.

'I'm afraid not,' Albert replied, 'you know what he was like. To be honest for all we know it might be a fish supper. Let's face it he wasn't a chap known for having a serious nature, but if there is something there and this storm has made it vulnerable to others we should do something about it.'

Norris breathed in heavily through his nose. He often did this as a prelude to a decision.

'I suggest that we examine the extent of the damage to the churchyard and then check with the parish records to see which graves have been affected and which ones are in danger of being next,' he said.

'I could get a long range weather forecast, see if further storms are expected,' Alf added.

'Why don't we just ask?'

Norris and Alf looked quizzically at Albert.

'If those chaps are from the council,' he indicated the men at the far table, 'they'll have probably gone over all of that.'

He shifted in his chair, the scrutiny of Norris and Alf was a little more attention than he was comfortable with.

'Why would they tell us anything?' Norris asked

'Why wouldn't they?' Albert replied. 'I mean, it's not a missile silo we're talking about here.'

Norris looked to Alf for some reassurance that Albert's idea was unworkable but his colleague simply raised his eyebrows and shrugged.

Albert took a sip of his tea and then stood, 'I'll go and ask.'

Before either man could comment Albert was on his way to the table of black jacketed men. They watched as the little man stopped and introduced himself, he shook the hand of the gent nearest to him and a conversation that neither of them could quite make out took place. A minute or so later Albert made his way back to the table and sat.

'Well,' he began, 'it appears that a good twenty feet of the coastline fell into the sea and a further ten feet is considered 'at risk.' They are also very worried about the met office's report that a substantial area of low pressure is forming in the North and that it may carry another strong period of stormy weather down onto the coast.'

Norris and Alf looked on, astonished.

'The young man on the side of the table nearest us is in charge of the works, and his name is Darren.'

A small smile crept along his mouth, hidden by his moustache. 'He's from Kent,' he added.

There was a moment's silence that was broken by Norris slapping his hand down on the table. 'Well done Albert, top hole,' he guffawed.

Alf grinned and patted Albert on the back, 'Good show Albie,' he said.

Albert was as happy as he had been in quite a while and continued drinking his tea, with a smile barely disguised by his moistened moustache.

The mood was now lifted a little in the group, especially as the news that 'Darren,' the Project Manager had delivered indicated that the situation was not one of imminent disaster. Twenty feet of eroded churchyard was, at present, tolerable, but the possibility of further collapse was still worrying.

After their tea was finished they decided to split up, each was to perform a set task, or number of tasks, and to meet again in the evening.

Norris would visit the museum. The custodian there was 'difficult' and as the tact of Alf and the reason of Albert rarely had any effect upon him they relied on the crowbar approach of Norris in any dealings with him.

Albert's mission was to check that the information he had gleaned from the gents at the Tea Room was accurate and that there were no other obvious problems at the churchyard.

Alf meanwhile was to visit various concerns in the area that might have some influence or agenda in the goings on at the church.

They all drove, but Norris and Albert had chosen to perform their assignments on foot, each destination being only a short walk through the town, but Alf required his car, an immaculate Triumph Roadster, as he had a number of locales to observe and people to interrogate.

Cars like Alf's were not uncommon in Whitby. A large portion of the demographic was both aged and wealthy and the three of them lived well within that portion of the regions wealth table. For any person or official body interested in their financial circumstances it would appear that they had each been blessed with successful stock market investments and sound property purchases at every step of their lives.

That not one of them had ever stepped foot into an estate agent's or actually understood how the stock market worked was something that other people did not need to know. Some jobs had perks and this was one of theirs.

***

Albert stood behind the red and white tape that cordoned off the unsafe area of land on the very edge of the churchyard. He marvelled at how, overnight, such a large chunk of land had simply disappeared into the sea. He didn't know if any of the headstones had been removed from the edge by the council workers but what was now the new perimeter was free of them for another eight feet or so. He estimated that the storm must have claimed at least forty burial sites.

He tightened his scarf and drew the collar of his jacket up. The churchyard was situated above the town and a very strong wind blasted across the waves and bit into the coast. Albert lifted his gaze to the swelling North Sea and wondered if it really was going to re-commence its assault on the town.

'Most likely,' he thought.

He had been surprised that the photographers from the newspapers had already left, but he also supposed that unless the church itself was to tumble into the sea there wouldn't be more to add to what they had already written.

Whitby was already old news. Albert thought it was probably better that way. Who really knew what might happen next? The harsh truth was that even they had no idea what could happen.

Sure enough the paper had set them all off at the same time. Alf called it their 'spider-sense,' the tingling feeling that danced across their skin whenever there was a threat of the sort that required their particular attention. Albert had thought that it was an awfully good description until he realised that Alf had gotten it from a comic book.

The problem, or one of the problems with the spider-sense, was that they had no clue as to what it might be. Also, it might be that one of them, sometimes all of them, but this was rare, that would get insights, flashes of inspiration that to a certain extent guided them to the problem, but there was never any consistency to it except that it was always something bad or at least intolerably weird.

To Albert the newspaper article had been like a bullhorn in his ear. None of them had realised the immense damage that the storm could do when the weather chaps had warned it was coming, but as soon as they had each seen the headline this morning their skin had felt like a million icy cold needles had begun to dance over it. Whatever it was it was going to be, all of them agreed, it was going to be very bad.

Norris pushed open the door of the museum, ignoring the 'Closed' sign that was clearly placed in the middle of it, and strode inside. The museum was supposed to be locked up, shut for the winter but this was never the case. It was also supposed that the 'custodian,' or Museum Associate as the label embroidered on his mauve lab coat announced, was also supposed to be away for the same period, doing whatever it was seasonally employed people did when the season ended. This was also not something that happened.

This man was as much a fixture of the museum as the huge skull of the Sperm Whale hanging from the ceiling above tourist's heads as they milled around the place.

Whitby Museum was typical of its kind, an aged but heavily renovated building. This one, constructed in the nineteen thirties, was filled with rusty relics and large storyboards telling the history of the town and its area. Glass cabinets ran the length of three long rooms containing all manner of items from the old days of the town's whaling industry. Almost every wall was obscured by paintings and almost all of them of a nautical nature.

As Norris walked briskly down the length of the room, directly ahead of the entrance, his cane tapped with every other step. The custodian looked up from the item he had been scrutinising and blinked at Norris with his heavily lidded eyes.

He was a strange looking man by anyone's opinion. Short, about five foot three, but with a solid almost cylindrical body hidden under a pale brown lab coat. His neck appeared to have no real contour, it was just a solid block up to the rest of his head. His hair was thin and black, waxed back, possibly, but it could as easily be just very greasy.

Under his almost non-existent eyebrows were heavy eyelids and recesses from which his eyes bulged as though his head was being squeezed between giant fingers. From there a flattened nose led to a turned down, thin-lipped mouth.

Norris stopped a couple of feet away from the little man.

'I like what you have done with your hair Phillip,' he said.

'What do you want Norris?' Phillip replied with impatience, as he placed the item he was holding, something made of brass with little wooden pegs hanging from it, back into an open cabinet.

'I just need to know what's going on with the churchyard,' Norris replied.

'Going on?' Phillip said questioningly, his face attempted a 'what are you talking about' expression that unfortunately came across as 'I need the toilet' whenever he tried it.

'Don't mess about Phillip,' Norris snapped, instantly changing his tone, 'I need to know if there is a threat likely to come from the events at St. Mary's,' he took a step closer. 'This is as important to you as it is to us, understand?'

Phillips throat moved as he swallowed deeply, producing a sound not unlike a croaked hum.

'Hmm...I suppose,' he said. 'What has been damaged?'

'As far as I'm aware about twenty feet of the northern part of the cemetery and a further ten feet is under threat of collapse.'

'Ooh, that is quite a lot isn't it,' Phillip responded, genuinely impressed.

'Yes it is Phillip,' Norris said, 'and we need to know if there is anything to be concerned about if that last ten feet should break away.'

'Yes, indeed! There could be any number of embarrassments uncovered,' Phillip nodded, but as he didn't really have a neck for his head to hinge upon he achieved it by moving his upper body backwards and forwards.

'Come with me,' he said, and turning, he kicked at a panel that was out of Norris's view. A moment later there was a sound of a bolt or locking mechanism activating, it came from the front door. In another moment a small section of the wall opposite him began to slowly recede, taking with it the glass cabinet and portraits that adorned it.

This was no surprise or shock to Norris. He had seen it before.

***

Alf pulled up outside directly outside the Masonic Hall. He didn't worry about parking tickets. If ever he got one the little yellow slip on his windscreen would be all he would ever see of it. Somehow parking tickets received by Alf and his friends appeared to disappear into the ether. It was something that they had learned not to question. Another perk.

The Hall was one of the grandest buildings in Whitby, but it was set away from the main road and behind a formidable wall topped with wrought iron spikes. Beyond the double gates a gravel drive led up to the seventeenth century building. Tall columns reached to the second floor took position either side of a huge panelled door which was decorated with intricately carved symbols.

While Alf appreciated the buildings stately architecture he had no such appreciation of the people who inhabited it at the moment. Despite it being called the Masonic Hall it had not been the home of that particular group for some time. Instead it was home to a gathering even more secretive and of an even more dubious character.

There was no doorbell or intercom. Instead a large iron hoop pierced the mouth of a snarling beast of indeterminate species. Alf lifted it and let it fall. The deep thud of it against the strong panel resonated through the hall. The knock was answered within a few seconds.

The great door swung open slowly, as if its weight were so great that gravity was fighting its movement. Once it revealed sufficient space a figure appeared from within. He was dressed in a smart, but distinctly out of its time period, flannel suit. He was thin to the point of being skeletal and had an unhealthy hue to his complexion. A sharp nose and widow's peak suggested to Alf a rat like appearance.

'Mister Bradburn, what can we do for you today?' The rat-man asked.

'I need to know what's going on up at the Abbey,' Alf replied

'Going on?' Rat man returned.

'Is this something your lot are involved in? Because if it is I can guarantee that it's going to cause problems for everyone, not just us,' Alf fired at him.

Rat-man grimaced, 'Oh...you must mean the storm. Mister Bradburn I can assure you that we have had no part in any business or commotion at the Abbey. You know, sometimes when there is thunder it isn't Thor doing his parlour trick, it's just the weather.'

Alf nodded, 'Fair enough,' he looked about, checking for anyone who might be in earshot and then spoke in a lower tone. 'There has been ghoul activity recently too, nothing major, but we know there is a least one in the area.'

Rat-man pursed him lips and also performed a quick scan of the immediate vicinity, 'Yes, we are aware that there is a creature at large and we are already looking into the matter.'

'Well, look a little harder,' Alf said, 'that sort of stuff is your responsibility and I'll be damned if we are going to tidy up your mess again.'

Rat-man looked as though he were about to rebuke Alf's challenge but seemed to think better of it.

'Yes, of course, and we appreciate your help with that previous... uh, unpleasantness,' he said, scrawling a look of disingenuous gratitude on to his face.

Alf turned to leave, but was halted as rat-man tapped his shoulder lightly. Alf looked back at him. Rat-man had managed to achieve a different kind of smile that he assumed was supposed to be friendly. It was wide, and toothy, and quite awful.

'Could I ask what the problem is at the Abbey, I mean is it something that we at the Lodge should be concerned about?'

'No,' Alf replied, and continued his exit from the Hall.

'Uhm...' Rat-face called after him, 'no there is no problem?'

'No you can't ask,' Alf called back without pausing in his stride.

***

Darren Keats had been sat in his work van drinking what he estimated was his fifth, put possibly sixth cup of tea of the morning, when he spied the man who had spoken to him at the Tea Room walking up to the edge of the churchyard. As he sipped at his drink he found himself watching the old geezer with an intense interest that he couldn't explain.

Something about the little man wasn't quite right, but he couldn't put his finger on it. He seemed amiable enough. When he had approached them in the tea room he had been very polite and unassuming, a gent in fact. He had been curious about the problems with the coastline up at the church, which was understandable as he was almost certainly a local, yet... no, Darren couldn't quite place his unease. He lost sight of the old man as he crested the rise the drive took to the churchyard.

He gulped down the last of his lukewarm tea. It had cooled as he looked over the plans for fencing off the cliff edge, and putting in place a series of strong wire nets to help reinforce the crumbling surface. It was only temporary, everything he did was temporary these days. Flood relief, wind damage and dangerous structures all needed a man with his talents before anything else.

He was a fixer, but only a temporary fixer it seemed. After his team had erected their scaffolding, sandbagged the roads and distributed warning leaflets, they would move on, and the *real* guys would come and finish the job properly.

Occasionally it stung him a little. There was no doubt that he was in demand. At thirty-two he was the go-to guy for this kind of event and his salary reflected this admirably. He owned his house, a detached in Kent with an acre of land. He had a girlfriend of five years, Katie, who was both supportive of his long days away from home and who made him miss her during every one of them. But he had always wanted to build something amazing, rather than 'patch up' something that had been battered by any number of the elements.

He checked the manifest. He had ordered a couple of JCB earthmovers for today and neither had shown up. Something pinched at his thoughts,

'*Why do I need Earthmovers? ...for moving the earth of course...*'

Darren shook a little, dislodging the strange thought. He needed to call the local council office to find out what was going on with those vehicles, but he decided that first he would head up to the church and make final inspection of the storm damaged land. He also hoped to bump into the old man, he couldn't say why.

The old boy had been an odd sort but in amiable way. The little bow-tie and considerable moustache were charming in their antiquity and Darren thought that the guy must have the same stylist as Einstein, his white hair practically erupted around him. Yet the desire to meet him, to just chat, was almost palpable.

He exited his van and trudged up the drive to the churchyard. The wind was picking up and was bitterly cold. He buttoned over his collar on the thick donkey jacket but decided to leave his high-vis safety helmet behind. If the old fellow could manage without a hat so could he.

'*Diggers... digging in the ground...why don't you dig it?*' he thought momentarily, and again dismissed it from his mind, but also resolved to ease off on the morning caffeine intake.

When he reached the top he could see the man, his outline was unmistakable, stood by the safety tape. The brightly coloured line of plastic vibrated in the wind and by Darren's reckoning, if the cliff collapsed further, it wouldn't reach as far as the area he had marked out.

He had a momentary chill as his mind created a sudden rumble and the old man disappeared from view, falling into the sea.

He needed his brain to stop pulling little stunts like that, he was beginning to wonder if perhaps he had been working a little too hard lately.

The old man appeared not to notice his approach. Gusts of wind muffled his footsteps on wet, and now that he and his men had been busy on it, muddy grass.

'Hello again,' Darren called out.

The old man turned and didn't appear to be startled or at all surprised. A broad smile broke across his face. Darren thought he must have too smile a little harder than most because of the moustache.

'Why hello!' Albert replied, 'nice to see you again, its Darren isn't it?' he extended his hand.

Darren took it and they shook firmly, '*strong grip*' he thought.

'The storm did a fair job on it,' Darren said, returning his hands to the warmth of his pockets and nodding towards the cliff edge.

Albert turned back to the view, 'Yes, it's amazing. So much power, so much anger in the wind at the moment.'

Darren thought it an unusual, but apt description. The storms had been quite relentless, for England at least. This was the fourth coastal area he had come to manage in a month, although this was also the most unusual, he had dealt with flooded cemeteries before but never had one falling into the sea.

The two men now stood side by side. Darren towered above Albert. Most people did, and Darren was a six-footer like Norris. Albert mused that if he had Darren and Norris either side of him it would be like standing inside a well.

'Could I ask what will happen with the graves and bodies that have been 'scattered'?' Albert inquired.

'Oh, we'll hopefully collect everything up. The main man at the Whitby Lifeboat Service suggests that the shore here is very consistent. The current will bring anything that is dropped into the sea along this line of the coast, and apparently it ends up in the same place.' Darren said, 'The lads are starting this afternoon when the gear arrives.'

'Good, good' Albert said, 'and what about the 'protruding items,' and the graves that are under threat?'

'We're bringing in a team that we've used before. Professional climbers. They'll abseil down the cliff face and remove what they can,' Darren was careful not to use the term *remains*, 'after that we'll be digging up the whole area that you can see cordoned off. We will have to do this manually though, the weight and vibration of mechanical diggers might be too much for the cliff to bear.'

'*Diggers*,' the word kept buzzing around his thoughts.

'Exhumation?' Albert asked.

'Uh... oh... yes, afraid so,' Darren replied, 'the plan is to reinter the graves we move to the other side, landward of the church.'

'Sounds pretty solid to me, a good plan,' Albert said and gave Darren a reassuring smile.

'Yes. We think so. Minimum disruption. Safe, at least as safe as we can make it, and we should be done within two days.' Darren nodded to himself. It *was* a good plan.

'What if there is another storm?' Albert asked

Darren paused for a moment. He had considered this but the weather reports indicated nothing more serious than they were currently experiencing, at least for the next three to four days.

'More of the same to be honest... I'm sorry please forgive me but I've forgotten your name, I know you told me in the Cafe.'

'It's Albert, Albert English,' Albert offered his friendliest smile to set Darren at ease over his slight faux pas, 'I'm sure I only recall yours because I have a nephew named Darren in Worcestershire.'

'Thank you Albert. As I said, it's more of the same really. This cordon,' Darren pointed towards the plastic tape, 'represents where I would expect the collapse to reach should the cliff-face take the same, or even a greater hammering as it did the other night. We would simply perform the same operation. Also if it did occur I'm quite certain that this far back the rock is much more solid, and according to the tests we did yesterday, less porous than the earth ahead of it, so it would withstand a far stronger assault from the sea and wind.'

'Ah... good,' Albert said.

Darren couldn't be certain but it looked as though a genuine relief appeared on the old gent's face.

The two then men stood and looked out at the sea. In nautical terms it was choppy. The swell was above normal and appeared agitated, it was full of nervous energy and all along the coast waves slammed against the sand like the fist of an angry child.

'It terrifies me you know,' Albert said without looking away, 'the sea.'

Darren didn't know what to say to this. Obviously Albert had made his home here, why on earth would someone live by the sea if they were scared of it.

'Oh,' was all he could think to say.

After a further pause Albert said, 'Well...I should be on my way I suppose, time to meet with the lads.'

'Your friends from the Cafe?'

'Yes, that's them, the dynamic duo,' he extended his hand once again to Darren, who was a bit reluctant to remove his from the warmth of his pocket, 'It's been a pleasure Mr Keats.'

'Yes, a pleasure for me also Albert. Hopefully we will be out of your way within the next couple of days.'

He placed his warm hand into the cast iron grip of Albert and shook again. They said good-bye and Albert strolled off across the churchyard.

When Albert disappeared from view Darren reflected on his encounter. His first impression of him had been that he was a 'funny little old man,' but he reminded himself not to be so shallow and judgemental of people. It was remarkable to him, he had felt like a little boy up here, on the cliff, next to a man who appeared to command the area he stood in.

Even though it had been he answering all the questions, as the person with the knowledge, he felt that Albert was the wiser and knowing one. Perhaps it was an age thing.

'*It terrifies me, the sea.*'

That was odd. The statement stuck in Darren's mind but he couldn't say why. A blast of wind upset his balance a little but he shrugged it off.

'It won't get worse for a couple of days at least,' the Met boys had said. It was cold though. Bitter. He turned from his view of the restless sea and went back to the van to chase his diggers.

'*Baby can you dig your man...*' the thought, a song lyric?

Where the hell did that come from? Was that... Stephen King? Darren decided he was done with coffee for the day.

***

They had agreed to rendezvous at Giuseppe's at five o' clock. Albert was the closest to it and had the simplest job to do, made even easier by his chance meeting with Darren. He was now confident that the issue of the cliff-face was sorted. He arrived at four and found the Tea Room empty. While he waited for the others to arrive he had Giuseppe make him a bowl of homemade soup that was the Sicilians own recipe, it was quite excellent. Tomato with bacon pieces with a variety of complimentary herbs.

'Bloody tractors come by earlier,' Giuseppe said as he placed the steaming, fragrant bowl down in front of Albert.

'Do you mean earthmovers... uhm... diggers?' Albert asked

'Yeah, that's it. Diggers. Bloody Diggers come by, making the big row, like bloody tanks.' Giuseppe said with his usual reproach. 'I not seen the church yet. Is it bad?'

'The church? The church is fine, it's the Abbey, and it's just the edge of the graveyard Giuseppe. And yes, it is quite bad really, about ten feet has fallen away and there is a possibility of a further section collapsing too.'

Giuseppe crossed himself with the hand that held his teacloth and then he kissed the edge of it.

'Is a bad business for sure,' he said, 'I read the papers and they says there's skulls and bones on the shore.'

'Well, it was only the one skull Giuseppe, a very old one I believe. No one has been buried at the church for over a hundred years.'

Albert was well aware that this was not entirely true but it was not something that Giuseppe, or anyone else needed to know.

'Yeah well, still it's a bad business,' Giuseppe said, utterly unmoved by Albert's compromise. The two said nothing for a moment. 'Where's your home boys?' Giuseppe asked.

'Excuse me?' Albert said

'My son says it all the time, he's, 'out with his home boys,' something to do with black people I think. I don't know.'

'Oh right,' Albert frowned a little, not sure if a comment like that constituted being racist these days, 'They are coming shortly, I'm early.'

'Ok, for sure.' Giuseppe responded, 'You think they want soup?'

'I... don't really know. Possibly, I suppose.'

'I make up some soup,' Giuseppe said, and then promptly left the table, disappearing into the kitchen.

Something nibbled at Albert's thoughts. During the conversation with Giuseppe the feeling he got when there was something wrong, something at odds with how he had perceived things, had come to him and it was pinching at his spine.

Alf entered. He made his way directly to Albert and sat in his usual chair.

'Where is he?' Alf asked.

'Who? Giuseppe?

'No, Basil Fawlty,' Alf snapped.

'I say,' Albert said, 'there's no need for that, you could have meant Norris.'

Alf puffed out a long breath, 'Sorry. Not a good afternoon.'

Albert didn't press it. An apology sincerely meant was enough for him to forget almost any slight.

'Oh dear, the Lodge?'

'No, not the Lodge. For once I don't think they've had their creepy little fingers in this one,' he looked at the empty bowl in front of Albert. 'Is there any more of that?'

'Giuseppe is just making some up now.'

'Good.' Alf said and began to remove his coat. 'No Albie, after the lodge I went to see Old Moll.'

'Oh,' Albert said in a manner that did not attempt to hide his disgust.

'Yeah, yeah,' Alf agreed, 'but she knows stuff Albie, she knows all those things that the lads who got us into all this never thought to tell us.'

'I can't argue with that Alf but really, was there no other option?'

'Not unless we start reading the books Albie, and we both know where that can lead,' he raised his eyebrows.

'Yes... I suppose we do,' Albert replied with resignation. 'What did the old cow have to say?'

'Well first off she went on a huge rant about the council and the change in bin collection days. I don't think I have ever heard so much foul language come from one mouth.'

'She does have a way with words,' Albert agreed.

'However, she did suggest that there could be a problem at St Mary's.'

'Oh?' Albert was all ears.

Alf craned his neck around to see if Giuseppe might be at the door to his kitchen. He couldn't see him. He lowered his voice to a whisper.

'Aye, it seems our 'feeling' definitely wasn't just because of the weather.'

Their heads moved together a little and Alf brought up his hand to obscure his mouth.

'There is something in one of the graves that is very, very bad news if it gets disturbed.'

'What is it?' Albert asked in an excited whisper.

'I don't know,' Alf replied.

'Where about is it?'

'I don't know,'

'Well, what will it do?' Albert pressed.

'I'm not sure.' There was silence for a moment then Albert straightened a little, Alf followed suit.

'So, we don't know what it is, where it is or what it does, but there is something that is very, very bad news up at St. Mary's.'

'In a nutshell, yes,' Alf replied.

'I'm not sure that could be any more vague,' Albert remarked, 'I hope you didn't pay old vinegar tits for this amazing information.'

'Of course I paid her. You don't just ask questions of a witch and then not pay her.'

Albert shook his head, 'Honestly Alf, I expected better from you... a witch.'

'Look, it does one thing,' Alf raised his index finger, 'it confirms what we all felt. That there is a danger at the church and a substantial one at that.'

At this the door to the Tea Room opened and Norris appeared in the doorway. He looked pale. Like Alf he scanned the room for people other than his friends and then made his way directly to them. He sat.

'Where is he?' Norris said.

'He's in the kitchen making soup,' Albert replied.

'Right. We have a big problem,' Norris said and added, '*very* big.'

'The church?' Alf said.

Norris nodded, 'Yes. The churchyard, of course, as we suspected'

'Is it ghouls?' Albert asked the question in a hopeful tone. Ghouls were fairly easy to deal with, once you found their nest.

Norris slowly shook his head, 'No. It's not Ghouls.'

He looked around again before stating clearly and gravely.

'A Chthonian.'

Alf and Albert looked at him with calm, cool eyes, and in tandem asked,

'What's a Chthonian?

'Right, of course, you don't know. Sorry I just... right. Its big, and I mean bloody huge. It...'

Giuseppe burst through the door from the kitchen. Seeing the three friends now gathered he stretched his arms in welcome.

'Ahh, here we all are again! The Mooseketeers return.' Giuseppe ambled over and pointed at Norris.

'You look like you could use some of Giuseppe's Tomato soup eh?'

'Oh... no, I mean yes... yes I'll have soup. Thank you.'

'I'll take a bowl as well please Giuseppe.' Alf added so that Giuseppe would be finished at the table sooner.

'Bene, bene. I be back real soon. You want drinks while you wait?'

'Tea.' The three answered as one.

'Ok, three teas as usual. I'll be right back.' He slung his tea cloth over his shoulder and returned to the kitchen.

Albert and Alf returned their attention to Norris.

'So what's a Chthonian?' Alf said, 'Is it in the book?'

'Not our book,' Norris replied, 'Phillip's book.'

'I knew that little weirdo had something in that museum,' Alf said. 'He knows full well he isn't allowed to keep anything Eldritch in a public place.'

'I don't think the public will be finding that place to be honest Alf. And I'm not sure we would have this information if Phillip had not deemed it so important to us.' Norris said, in his gravest tone, 'If this thing comes to Whitby it will be a disaster, a catastrophe. This is not a ghoul, or goblin or some lesser thing that has stumbled through a portal those clowns at the lodge have conjured up.'

'Good Lord!' Albert exclaimed

'Yes... Good Lord indeed,' Norris said as he leaned back and spread his hands as though to offer some indication of scale, but after a moment of moving them in and out gave up. 'Lads this is a monster, a true monster. I've only seen an artists rendition of one of them, and a few photographs of areas where they are thought to have surfaced.'

He placed his hands flat on the table. 'Gentlemen, if this thing is called to Whitby the entire town will be wiped off the face of the map.'

'All for one and a one for all!' Giuseppe shouted as he emerged from the kitchen. He carried a large tray featuring three vast bowls of soup, a number bread rolls that looked like heavily tanned hamsters and three mugs of tea with, 'I love Whitby,' printed around them. He almost shimmied to the table.

'Here you go guys, Giuseppe's famous tomato soup. Best in all Sicily, and now all Whitby.'

Once he had finished placing the bowls and mugs he stood at the edge of the table, slinging the towel he used to prevent the hot bowls from burning his fingers jauntily over his shoulder. He smiled at the men, who he had not noticed until now, looked glum and turned to view the rest of the Tea Room.

'Hey. Why it so fucking quiet in here?' he said.

***

Phillip was nervous. Not because he had shown Norris the books, he was certain he had done the right thing in that respect. He couldn't deny the fact that as big a pain in the arse the three of them were they did keep the town safe. More importantly to him they also tolerated his condition, and the activities of some of the other individuals and groups in the area, that others would certainly not let slide, at least not without pitchforks, fiery torches and a lot of yelling.

In return, every now and then they needed to be advised of some eldritch lore or the more practical side of things, and they would come to see him, and every time he helped his continued presence in the town was maintained.

Despite his loathing of the tourists that came to the museum, and the townsfolk generally, and his grudging mostly one-sided relationship Norris and the other old sods, he was at home in Whitby. By his own estimate he had no more than another five years before the change was complete and he could return to his other home, his true home.

He hoped he would be welcomed by the great Father on the shore, and be able to join him on the long swim. Phillip found it difficult to blink these days as his eyes had begun to bulge so much, but when he thought of that day coming he needed to do it, to move the tears that welled in his glassy eyes.

It was all very nice to think about, unless he got stationed by the Elders in some shithole like Scotland, again. His already naturally turned down mouth arched even further. He had lived in Scotland for a while, in a remote port town and that had not ended well at all. Fires, bullets, explosions and finally… he shuddered.

He had been lucky to escape in one piece and find himself able to settle here in Whitby.

Upon arrival he had sought out the most likely places to find his kind. Places where being 'odd' and having unattractive features didn't matter so much. Art galleries, museums, fast food restaurants. It had to be by the sea, naturally, and so this meant enduring the seasonal swarm of mindless oaf's looking to drink themselves into oblivion in the evening and acquiring skin cancer on the beach during the day, where they slept through the inevitable alcoholic coma.

His luck at escaping that awful Scottish town had stayed with him since his flight along the coast. The curator of the Whitby museum was one of his own kind. Almost at the point of returning.

His name was Alick, and he was so close to his change that he no longer dared be seen in public. Instead he had brought in one of the morons from the Lodge to run the place, while he sat in the shower at his home.

Alick had been very glad to see Phillip arrive, but the Lodge mook wasn't, as his services were no longer required. Most likely he had been hoping to discover Alick's secret room and the contents therein. Those Lodge bastards only ever did things to serve themselves.

A fuss had been made and unpleasantness had ensued. In the end they had called in the Guardians to sort it out, and the mook had gone running back to the lodge. Finally, when Alick returned to the Great Father, Phillip took his place officially.

He enjoyed working at the museum. Cataloguing, cleaning and maintaining the exhibits relaxed him. This was ruined by visitors, but by avoiding any advertising whatsoever and leaving the door shut, but unlocked, people mostly assumed the museum was closed unless they took the effort to try and come in.

Phillip couldn't be more unhelpful if he tried, and added to this were his strange and unappealing looks which tended to make people want to leave in a hurry anyway.

His concern now was that if the Guardians failed to sort out this new threat none of all that would matter. The town would be gone, utterly ruined and he would be off again, looking for work, looking for a new home until his time came. Better to show off a few dark secrets than have to try and exist in the hateful world beyond Whitby.

However, he couldn't rely on them succeeding and had begun to pack because he was nothing if not pragmatic and even if he wanted to help he wasn't sure that he could. To begin, he didn't think he could drive anymore. His hands were far too clumsy in their present form and his feet were not particularly responsive. He was immensely strong but that was no use if you couldn't walk worth a damn.

Thus he was limited to what he could realistically take with him. He could probably *carry* a car yet he couldn't take even half of the items he wished to keep. He would have to bury them. Somewhere the Lodge wouldn't go sniffing and somewhere that the lecherous old trout Molly wouldn't be sending her little helpers.

'*Warlocks and witches,*' he thought, '*Scum.*'

***

After finishing their soup and mugs of tea Norris, Albert and Alf headed to the churchyard, this time as a group. The town was quiet. Giuseppe had been right to bemoan the lack of custom but it seemed that no one, not a soul was out and about in Whitby this evening.

'No one in the streets,' Alf said, 'that's not a good sign.'

'A spell you think?' asked Norris

'Probably not,' Albert said, 'When there is substantial Aetheral activity people tend to stay indoors through pure instinct, they will work, go the theatre and even enjoy a party, but something keeps them indoors. I bet they'll scamper home tonight after their shifts are done. Dogs won't even want a walk.'

'I think you're right Albie, you can feel it a little... the oppression in the air. It's like the Earth is standing still.'

They approached the entrance to St. Mary's. A wall all around parted for a driveway that led up and over the rise to it.

Suddenly Albert stopped and cried out, 'DIGGERS!'

It caught Norris and Alf completely by surprise. They too both halted and stared hard at the little man.

Albert slapped his hand against his head.

'The lad Darren, the project manager, he said that they would not be using diggers because it could cause the land to subside. So why had he arranged to hire diggers?' Albert began to talk quickly, 'Why did diggers drive past the Tea Room today?'

He waved his finger at the church, 'What is being dug up at St. Mary's and why?'

He almost yelled it.

'Dear God,' said Norris. 'We had better get a move on.'

They advanced upon the churchyard as fast as they could but didn't dare break into a run. Residents who witnessed three men in their nineties sprinting into a churchyard would ask questions. Fingers would be pointed. As it was their job as Guardians to ensure that fingers remained on TV remotes and Smartphones they were discreet in revealing the abilities they had, beyond looking and moving 'well for their age.'

When they reached the top of the grounds, where the path started to wind its way around the church and accompanying cemetery, they saw two large, bright yellow earthmovers. Their scoops were raised. Drivers sat inside, motionless.

Albert could see Darren. He was sat, legs out, with his back resting against a headstone.

'Look, it's Darren,' he said, and ran ahead, now unconcerned if he was seen. He suspected that the weirdness people might experience was not about to get stranger just because he was seen to pelt down the path.

Norris and Alf chased after him. Norris's flat cap almost left his head as a blustery bout of wind met them.

When Albert reached Darren he got to one knee and looked the boy over. He appeared to be asleep, not dead. His arms were at his sides, empty hands flat on the floor. He had his big coat on but no hat or gloves.

'Poor boy,' Albert said, 'you must be freezing.'

He had a woollen hat in his pocket which he took out and pulled over the unconscious Project Managers head. He pushed Darren's cold hands into pockets of his jacket.

Norris and Alf stood over Albert.

'Is he injured,' Alf asked.

'Not that I can see,' Albert replied.

He moved a hand to Darren's face and lifted each eyelid in turn, 'He's been mesmerised.'

'Are you sure?' Norris asked.

'Pretty sure,' Albert replied, 'I'll wager those lads aren't so lucky.'

He looked up toward the digger operators. Alf and Norris walked over to the cabs and each checked an occupant. Alf studied the face of the man in his cab. In the poor light it was difficult to be sure but the driver's pudgy face was pale and his lips appeared to have a blue tint to them.

He climbed down and called to Norris, 'Hypothermia?'

Norris spent a few more moments examining his chap. A young man, younger than Darren, his face was slack and pale. He also saw a bluish colouring on this man's lips but there was also a trace of foamy spittle.

'Poison,' Norris answered as he stepped away. 'I'm not sure how it was administered but I'm fairly certain that's what did for him.'

They turned their attention to the large hole that had been excavated by the dead men.

Norris walked over to it while Alf stayed back and looked out for anyone or anything that was moving or made as if to move.

Peering into the hole Norris could see to the bottom of the great brown maw that had been created. There, smashed beyond recognition was what had once been a crypt. A rope led into it, fixed above ground to the bumper of the digger to his right.

He called back to Alf and Albert.

'They broke into a crypt, a deep one. Looks like they dug down to it and then smashed the roof with the diggers.'

He took his torch and shone it into the ruins below. The masonry that had once been the ceiling had been broken up to leave a sizable entrance. Some of it had been torn out by the digger scoops and deposited in the piles at the side of them. Some had dropped down into the crypt itself. His eyes followed the length of rope into it but he could see nothing but the cold grey floor reflected in the powerful torchlight.

'Looks like they climbed in,' Norris shouted. The wind was really picking up and he found himself struggling to be heard.

'Do you think they found it in there?' Alf shouted back, 'the relic.'

Norris looked out across the churchyard and to the cliff edge where the sky beyond had darkened in no way that could be described as natural.

'Yes. I would say they did,' he replied. He didn't bother shouting this. Alf and Albert were now both looking out at the patch of purple-black darkness that was spreading towards them. As one they reached into their pockets and each man withdrew a pistol, they checked their guns were loaded and ready to be fired.

***

'Candles,' Phillip said, again. 'I just want candles.'

He was well aware that his voice was a little phlegmy and had a strained sound, almost a croak to it, but he was fairly sure that the long haired youth that had 'Chris' embossed onto his 'Best Home DIY' badge was taking the piss.

'So you want four candles,' Chris said, grinning and revealing extremely unflattering braces.

'Look I don't care how many there are... well no, I do, I need at least half a dozen I suppose, but could you just give me a pack of them. If they come in fours that's fine, I'll take two packs.' Phillip said carefully and as clearly as he could.

Chris continued to display his brace laden grin. 'Do you want any O's?'

'What?' Phillip asked with incredulity.

'Do you need any O's with your candles?' Chris said, his face was now starting to turn a little crimson with the laughter he was suppressing.

'No,' Phillip replied with as much force as he could muster. 'I do not require any hose.'

'Candles it is then,' Chris said. He sauntered off across the shop floor. His shoulders moved up and down as giggles took him and he struggled to keep them in check.

Shortly, he re-appeared around the corner of an aisle carrying a small box. He still had his large, stupid smile but the braces had retracted. Phillip glared at him.

He paid for the candles with a worn five pound note and as the store assistant went about performing his cash register routine he decided that if he had to opportunity to save 'Chris' from the disaster that was about to befall Whitby, he wouldn't.

'There you go sir,' Chris said handing out change on top of a crisp white receipt.

Phillip noticed that an older lady had appeared nearby, dressed in similar apparel and sporting a badge like Chris's but that had a little row of gold bars underneath it.

'*Most likely his supervisor,*' he thought. No wonder the boys strange and pointless questions had stopped. The lad then handed over his pack of a dozen candles which Phillip placed into the large leather holdall he wore at his side.

'Have a nice evening,' Chris said without any sincerity. Phillip didn't reply.

He shuffled out of the store and into the empty street. It was dark already. It wasn't supposed to be dark yet. He looked towards the church up on the hill. It loomed. Buildings always seemed to loom when it was dark and bad times were coming.

He sighed, gurgled a little, and began to shuffle as quickly as he could towards it.

***

'What do we do now?' Albert asked as they gathered around Darren's unconscious body to protect him from the worst of the wind.

'We need to get this lad out of the way for a start, he'll die of pneumonia and that's if nothing else gets to him first,' Alf said.

'Aye,' said Norris reaching down and grasping Darren's arm. Alf took the other and between them they lifted him effortlessly to standing.

Albert stepped away to give them room to move.

'Of course you know that whoever took that relic is going to want to use it immediately,' he said.

'Yes,' Alf agreed, 'they know we are on to them most likely, hence the rush to do this tonight.'

The wind was pushing at his back as he and Norris walked on with the suspended Darren hanging limply.

'And if they are in a rush where do you think the obvious place would be to perform the summoning?'

Alf and Norris stopped and turned to look at the church.

'I suppose it makes sense,' Alf said, and as he looked up at it a brilliant light illuminated every window from within. It shone gloriously in the strange twilight.

'This just gets better,' said Norris.

They moved as quickly as they could without causing injury to Darren towards the entrance of the church. Once there, Albert carefully pushed at the great studded door. It opened slowly. He looked to the others. Norris nodded. Albert pushed it open a little further.

The door didn't lead directly into the main chamber, instead there was a large foyer with another door ahead. They moved inside and laid Darren down upon one of two cushioned benches that faced each other on either side of the room.

Around the edge of the furthest door the light that had lit up the windows also beamed through the gap between it and the frame.

'They must be quite far through the ritual if they have produced Aetheral light,' Alf said quietly, so as not to be heard past his friends.

Norris nodded and whispered, 'that Relic must be incredibly charged to be so quickly activated, we have to act now'

'Wait!' A voice from behind them barked out.

The three turned as one and directed their guns squarely at the source.

'Phillip?' said Norris.

***

Phillip stepped in from the howling wind and let the door slowly close behind him.

'What the hell are you doing here?' Alf demanded.

'I've bought candles,' Phillip replied, 'More than four if that makes a difference.'

He waited for a moment to see if he could glean any relevance. Satisfied that there was none he continued 'and some snake blood.'

Norris raised his eyebrows, 'It's a Silurian Ritual?'

Phillip performed his bow that served as a nod. Understanding that now was not the time to ask questions of how, what and why, the three accepted the candles Phillip presented to them. He then produced two vials which upon later inspection would prove to be Sarsens vinegar bottles. Vials were expensive apparently.

'I can't manage the words,' Phillip said.

'I can do it,' Albert replied taking both vials.

He grasped each candle in turn and uttered harsh, strange sounds through gritted teeth. He closed his eyes as he rolled each candle in his palms once, then knelt and placed them in a row on the floor.

Norris and Phillip watched all this as Alf kept his attention on the door. If anyone or anything were to open it he was ready to empty his gun into whatever it was.

No one saw Darren open his eyes.

He had begun to come around as he had been laid down upon the bench. His head was swimming and though coming to he could not move his body at all. It was as though his limbs were separate from his brain and its signals couldn't reach them. He had heard the three old men talk about a ritual, and then the 'other' had entered. There was more talk of rituals, and of fork handles. It was at that point that he had been able to open his eyes.

The room he was in, what he saw of it, told him that he was inside the church. The cushioned benches, the flowers and brass plaques, the large blocks of stone that made up the walls and the decorated tiles on the floor. He knew, somehow, that they had brought him here for his safety, but that there was also still great danger. A tingle began to dance up and down his spine.

Albert continued to whisper words over the candles and as he did so he took the vial and began to shake the contents liberally over them. The snake blood, *'lord knows where Phillip gets such stuff'* Albert thought, was heavily diluted with water and infused with various herbs. He could smell an acridity in the liquid as he doused the candles, which he thought might be Sarsens vinegar.

'It's done,' Albert said finally.

'What's done?' Darren said in a dozy, slurred voice.

All four pairs of eyes turned to him.

Darren blinked as he looked up at them. He had still not managed to gain the use of his arms or legs but could feel the connections rebuilding.

'Darren,' said Albert, 'are you alright? How do you feel?'

'I'm... I'm fucked,' he replied, 'I can't move.'

Albert moved over to him and was about to pat him on the arm until he realised that his hands were covered in the snake blood and herb cocktail.

Alf joined him by the bench.

'Listen to me carefully Darren, I literally do not have time to explain what is happening so I need you to just stay here. If you find you can move, then get out as fast as you can, and do go as far as you can.'

'Look, sorry to be a pain but you really need to do whatever it is you are going to do,' Phillip croaked, 'Do you have a plan?'

'Do you know what is behind that door Phillip? Who is doing this?' Alf asked.

'No. I'm sorry, but I just don't know. If there had been more time...'

'OK,' Alf said, 'the plan is that we open the door and shoot at anything standing, sitting, praying, chanting or in the act of doing something that even closely resembles weird.'

'Agreed,' Norris and Albert whispered in unison.

'If it's a Silurian Ritual we know they will have a fire pit,' Norris said, 'the creature they are trying to summon is enormous and I mean really, really big, so the pit will be sizable. We need to toss the candles into it. The more we can get into the fire the more it will spoil the ritual. What they are calling will begin to diminish in power and size, we may even be able to stop it completely.'

Norris turned to Phillip, 'You have done your bit Phillip, if you want to leave now, do so, and no one will think any worse of you.'

Phillip looked at the three with his bulging unblinking eyes.

'See ya,' he said, and shuffled out of the church.

Norris, Albert and Alf watched him go and the door swing shut behind him.

'OK. I admit that I misjudged the outcome of that offer,' Norris said.

'Right, its time,' Alf called to them, he was stood by the door. He hadn't been able to hear chanting up until now, but there it was, a droning, repetitive hum.

The others turned to face the door, pistols raised. As they did so the light that had been shining through the gap suddenly extinguished.

'Oh dear,' Albert said.

'Go!' Alf shouted. He reached for the handle and pulled open the door.

It wasn't quite as dark as they had expected inside, as a red hue hung about the interior. In the middle of the chamber, the pews had been cleared to the sides, a pit had been excavated and a glowing pile of embers pulsed within it. The light from it cast a crimson bloom around its circumference revealing robed figures with their arms stretched up, hands spread. They moved side to side, slowly, and a low sonorous hum filled the air.

True to the plan the three began to fire at the figures. The first round of shooting proved fatal to three of the worshipping figures, they dropped to the floor where they stood, but there were at least eight visible in the room and those remaining reacted in time to avoid the onslaught. They moved with lightning speed and disappeared into the shadows.

From the farthest point in the chamber a voice called out in a strange tongue. The language was one that the men had faint knowledge of and upon hearing it they knew that their peril had not diminished at all. The voice commanded its followers to attack.

The first ambush was upon Albert who had been the last to enter the chamber. A figure leapt from the darkened corner nearest him. Albert turned with almost equal speed and fired twice into his assailant who instantly fell dead against him. The heavy cloth hood that had obscured his attackers face fell away. Dead eyes set within a beaked, snake-like head greeted him.

'YIG!' Albert shouted.

Both Norris and Alf heard Albert's warning clearly. If they were worshippers of the snake demon Yig they would be carrying daggers. Long twisted blades coated with a toxin that would kill them almost instantly should they receive a single scratch on bare skin. If they were actual Brood of Yig, rather than just some loathsome human follower, the lowly Servants, they would spit too, a noxious creamy substance that blinded a person on contact with their eyes.

Albert already knew that they were Brood, he pushed the creature away and peered into the half-light, seeing their form.

'They are Brood lads,' he called out, 'the real McCoy!'

He could see Alf ahead of him, walking carefully, looking for a target. Norris was harder to discern, almost at the centre of the chamber and near to the edge of the pit the cultists had created. Albert cautiously walked towards Alf.

At the edge of the pit Norris reached inside his jacket pocket and withdrew his candles, scanning the gloom of the church as he did so. The red glow and the intense heat haze of the pit obscured any sign of movement that he might have been able to detect, confusing the shadows. He tossed the candles into the pit.

The reaction was instant and more than he had expected. A roaring flame leapt upwards from the searing fire and Norris feared it might actually reach the roof of the church. If that happened they would have homicidal cultists, possibly a creature from another dimension, and burning timber and tiles cascading down upon them to make life extremely difficult.

Fortunately, the column of fire retreated before any damage could be done to the roof. Immediately following the flames retreat Alf could hear strained hisses and cries around him. The cultists knew what these men were here to do and didn't hesitate, they attacked as one.

Alf opened fire as two of them leapt for him. He caught one squarely in the chest with a couple of rapid shots, but before he could turn his pistol to the other it was upon him. He fell backwards with the creature on top and disappeared into the dark.

'Alf!' Albert cried out.

Further shots followed but these were ahead. Norris was blasting away at the Cultists as he moved further into the church. Albert knew that there would be a leader, a head priest who was conducting the ritual, he had to be Norris's target. He couldn't be sure if Norris had seen Alf fall but he understood that he would leave his friend's to fend for themselves, there was more at stake than the lives of any one of them.

Albert gritted his teeth and continued to step forwards, hoping to close the distance on Alf and also bring himself closer to the pit, but ready for another ambush.

There was a rumble. It was faint, but Albert could feel it through his shoes.

'*Oh God! It's coming,*' he thought.

Norris pressed on towards the pulpit. There was a noise reverberating around the church making difficult to hear, a deep bass that thrummed against his lungs. He wasn't sure if it was a spell being cast by the Priest or perhaps some effect of the ritual.

When a vibration rippled across the soles of his shoes he knew that time was now very much against them. Even if he they weakened the pit and took down the Brood's High Priest they might still be too late. He didn't dare look back.

He had seen Alf drop one of the creatures, but then be pushed over in a grapple with another, he had almost run back to help but he knew he couldn't. He was the man at the front, he had delivered his candles to the pit he now had to take down the Priest.

From the corner of his eye he caught the faintest hint of a shadow that billowed as a cloak might. He extended his arm and trained his aim a few inches to the left of where he had seen the outline and fired two shots. There was a satisfying thump immediately after.

As he brought the pistol around the pit roared once again. Alf or Albert had managed to infuse their candles into the pit.

'*Good lads,*' he thought.

He moved on, not looking back. Albert and Alf knew what they had to do and it was up to him to take out the Priest. The sudden bloom of light, as he wasn't facing it this time, had allowed him to see deeper into the church.

At the farthest end on the right, stood upon the organist's chair, he saw the priest. He was human, at least appeared to be. He wore the same large, voluminous cloak as his acolytes but in the brief moment of vision Norris could see that it was decorated with sigils, his hair was thick and festooned with feathers. Far too fancy for a mere follower.

The pillar of fire once again receded into the pit and his sight of the leader was gone. Norris pressed on.

The acolyte had come at Alf without its dagger in hand, which was fortunate for him as it had the upper hand as they rolled across the floor. When they came to a stop it was on top of him and it raked its fingers at his face. Its nails were like talons and gouged his cheek. Alf cried out as the wound burned but had the wit to bring his leg up, with the flexibility of a dancer, and hook his calf across its throat. He snapped his leg down and the snake thing was sent sprawling.

His pistol was gone. It had been sent skittering across the floor. Alf flailed his foot out and through good fortune caught the dazed acolyte across its temple further stunning it.

'Alf, behind you.' Albert's distinctive voice.

Instinctively Alf rolled to the side and a dagger stabbed against the stone floor causing sparks to fly from it. Two shots rang out and Albert's bullets punched through the side of the thing as it was illuminated by the light of the pit behind it.

Alf got quickly to his feet and spied his chance to infuse the candles. He dashed towards the pit, he didn't dare to miss, and almost at its edge tossed them into it.

He turned away as the flames surged upwards. Now they only needed Albert. He turned to look for the little man but couldn't see him.

'Albert!' Alf shouted as loudly as he could. He picked up the dagger that the acolyte Albert had dropped by him.

'Albert speak to me!'

'I'm here, I'm OK,' Albert's voice came from within the dark. He then stepped in to the light offered by the pit. 'I tripped over the damn body back there,' he said.

Alf smiled with relief. 'I think we got them all. Norris is going for the leader, get your candles in there quick.'

Albert pulled the candles out. He felt he was too close to the pit and took a step back so that the wall of flame would not scorch him. As he did this a scaled hand flashed out and snatched the candles from his grasp.

In shock the two men turned to see the bloodied acolyte that Alf had kicked away from him, the one he thought he had kicked into unconsciousness. It raised a dagger in its free hand. Its mouth opened and a hiss issued from it, a long sinewy forked tongue waved as the dagger was pulled back and then struck.

It had gone for the chest of Albert, a large target that it thought it couldn't miss.

But Alf had recovered from the surprise sooner than his friend. He leapt forward and pushed Albert out of the way causing the snake-man to strike at thin air. The acolyte screamed in a fury and slashed upwards with the dagger. The tip of the blade scraped across Alf's face lightly cutting the skin. Alf immediately felt the sensation of numbness in his cheek, it began to spread quickly across his face, his right eye rolled lazily in its socket.

'*I'm done,*' he thought, '*In seconds I'll be gone.*'

He lurched forwards and grabbed the acolyte in a terrific bear hug. Albert had picked himself up from the floor and saw Alf lift the snake-man bodily. Alf turned for a moment, his good eye looked directly at his friend.

A smile, as best as he could manage appeared on Alf's face. He twisted around and hurled himself and the hissing acolyte into the pit.

The embers once again became a furious beam of fire. It roared up to the ceiling as Albert could only stand and stare.

As abruptly as it had begun the column of flame ended. There was nothing to be seen of the acolyte or Alf inside the angry black and red circle of heat.

Shots rang out. Norris. Albert could barely see for the tears that stung his eyes but he started forwards to find him. As he walked on the vibration that he had felt earlier coursed through his feet but with far more intensity. The pit began to glow more noticeably. Another shot rang out.

Norris had tried to keep the position of the feathered man in his mind. His spatial awareness was no better than any normal man's. For all that they were never ill, had the fitness of a nineteen-year-old and aged slightly slower, they had no other strengths or powers. What they had was knowledge denied to other men and a lifetime of experience in which they had put it to use, but that was all.

Norris listened. He could hear words being chanted at speed by the Priest. He lifted his pistol towards the where he was convinced he had seen him. He raised the gun a little, to accommodate for the height that the organists chair had given. Then fired each shot in a steady, constant rhythm, allowing the pistol to drop a fraction after each recoil, until the clip was empty.

Once again there was the sound of a body falling to the floor.

The vibration came again. Stronger. Far more forceful. Norris looked at his feet. The stones had begun to shiver and particles of dust danced in the grooves.

'Too late,' he said to himself.

He wanted to check that the Priest was actually dead, not just clipped or stunned, but he knew there was no time. He turned, to head back to the others, and saw Albert coming towards him.

'We have to get out here right now,' he shouted to Albert. 'Where's Alf?' he looked about.

The gradual increase in brightness of the pit had begun to push the shadows away. Albert mouthed the words but couldn't make sounds.

Norris came to him, 'Albert are you alright, where's Alf?'

'He's gone,' Albert finally uttered, 'He's…'

'Gone?' Norris's face turned to an ashen pallor, 'he's dead?'

'He fought, with one of the snake-men, it took the candles. Alf…' Albert coughed into his fist, 'I think was Alf was cut by its knife, he threw himself into the pit and took the thing with him.'

'My God,' said Norris.

The floor began to shake violently. Norris grabbed hold of Albert to steady himself and the ground beneath them stirred.

'We were too late Albert,' Norris said.

'No,' Albert replied. 'We did *something*.'

Norris heard some resolve creep back into Albert's voice. 'Whatever they were trying to bring through surely can't make it now, there isn't enough power left, the relic is at the bottom of that pit and the infusions have reduced its strength.'

The earth shook again, even more violently than before. 'Then what the hell is that!' Norris said excitedly.

'I think, that although we reduced the strength of the portal, it doesn't mean that there isn't something less powerful that can use it.'

Albert had to shout loudly even with Norris right next to him. 'It's coming to the relic. We can't stop it coming through so we will have to stop it once it gets here.'

Norris nodded and shouted back, 'Right, OK... but what can do? We have no explosives and these things are huge, bullets won't touch it.'

'I might have something,' said a voice that was trying to bellow over the noise of the quake.

Norris couldn't believe that he had not seen Darren standing not more than five feet away from him. His attention had been so fixed upon Albert that he had failed to see the lad cloaked in the shadows.

'Darren!' Albert turned to him.

'Look, I don't know what the fuck is going on here, but I know that those aren't party masks.'

He pointed to the corpse of an acolyte, 'and I saw your mate jump into that fucking fire with one of them.'

Darren stepped forward into the dim light, 'So I know you are very serious people.' He spat on the floor as though there was something distasteful in his mouth, 'Those bastards did something to me, to the lads outside as well, so if I can help, I will.'

'Young man what you need to do is get out of here as fast as you can and do not look back. Don't stop until you are in the next county, in fact don't stop until you get home to Kent,' Norris said firmly.

'Fuck that,' Darren said. He stepped closer. Norris could see something in his expression, in his eyes, a steel that he had seen before, in his own friends. He nodded at the Project Manager.

'Alright, what can you help with?'

'Come with me,' Darren replied, then turned and walked back towards the foyer.

Albert looked in wonder at Norris, 'Do you think...'

'Yes,' Norris replied.

They followed Darren into the foyer and back outside of the church. He led them to the huge hole and pointed towards the diggers. 'Do you think that this monster of yours would feel one of those up its arse.'

Norris considered it for a moment. 'Possibly, if the thing is not too big yes.'

'You won't kill it with iron or steel,' Albert said, 'dimensional beings don't die like normal creatures, you can hurt it, annoy it certainly, but you won't kill it.'

'We don't need to kill it,' said Norris, 'we need to keep it inside the church long enough for the portal to collapse. If that happens, and it's near enough, it will be dragged back inside.'

'How long with this… portal stay open?' Darren asked

'Minutes at most,' Norris answered.

'And with the infusion we added to the pit it will be exceptionally unstable,' Albert added.

The ground began to shake again and this time the men staggered as the earth beneath them became like rubber.

'It's almost here, we have to move now,' Albert said.

'I can drive one of these, can either of you?' Darren said.

'I can,' Albert replied.

'Right, help me get the lads out and we'll fire them up,' he looked at Norris, 'Mister…'

'Norris,'

'Norris, could you drag the lads to somewhere that is even slightly safer than here?' Darren knew without a doubt that these men, these wrinkly old age pensioners could probably give him a run for his money in any gym.

'Aye, I can do that,' Norris replied.

'Right then, let's get to it.'

They pulled each of the digger operators out and lay them away from the open pit they had dug.

Darren fired up his digger and after taking a moment to familiarise himself with the controls Albert did the same. Darren pulled up to the side of Albert's digger and opened the cab door so that he could speak to him, Albert did likewise.

'What's actually going to come out that pit Albert?' he shouted, 'In layman's terms.'

'It's a Cthonian,' Albert replied, also having to shout over the diesel engines, 'Imagine a worm the size of… well I don't know how big it will be but it's going to be big, apparently they don't come in small or medium.'

'A big worm,' Darren said.

'Yes. A very big, very angry worm.'

Darren tapped the wheel of his digger with each of his fingers and tightened his jaw. Albert wondered if the last five minutes of Darren's resolve and tremendous acceptance of what was going on around him was about to crumble.

'Fair enough,' he said and closed the cab door.

The two watched the church roof begin to crumble. The stained glass windows exploded outwards. The diggers heaved as though they were barrels on a rough sea and from the gaping holes where sixteenth century stained glass had once been a deep crimson light began to pulse.

Norris had reached the entrance to the drive with the second operator when the windows had shattered. He could see the ground throughout the churchyard rise and fall, headstones tilted or fell flat, great statues toppled from their plinths and smashed to pieces upon the writhing floor. The pulsing glow suddenly grew more intense until in an instant it was eerily silent and utterly dark.

The headlights of the diggers came on and illuminated the church wall.

A sound broke the silence. An ungodly combination of a high pitched screech and a deep, stomach churning reverb that carried across the town, cutting at the nerves of those that heard it.

Dogs howled furiously, trying to drown out the sound and to offer what threat they could to the creature that issued the dreadful cacophony.

The walls of the church bulged impossibly and then broke with fury as an enormous bulk pressed at them. By the light of the diggers a pallid, pinkish wall of flesh became visible, just a small part of some enormous creature that was being born into this world was thrashing inside the church.

Debris was thrown up and outwards by the thing as it emerged. Foot thick timber joists and large clumps of masonry rained down upon the diggers.

Briefly Norris stared with fascination as the diggers moved into action but had to quickly dive behind a nearby wall as a rain of deadly pieces crashed around him.

Albert lowered the earthmovers bucket until it pointed straight out like a toothy lance. He waited for the thing to expose more of itself through the disintegrating wall and when a large patch of its hide appeared he revved the engine and stamped on the accelerator. The digger had a surprising kick and Albert was pulled back against the cab as it shot forward.

The teeth of the bucket hit the creature directly and managed to pierce its skin but the effect appeared to be unnoticed. Albert lifted his foot and then stamped down again to try and increase the pressure upon the bucket and further impale the creature.

Whether or not its current state of being born into the world prevented the monster from understanding that it was under attack he couldn't know, but it didn't attempt to swing around and retaliate. Albert decided to press his luck and continued to try and gain even more depth into its side.

Darren saw the lack of success that Albert was having and realised that the bucket would not be able to cut into the abomination any more than it had. The thing would twist around or even simply roll over and crush the digger, and Albert with it.

He reversed his vehicle a little and then drove it rapidly around to the entrance of the church. By his reckoning if the thing had a front then it was facing this doorway as it emerged from the portal.

He checked the structure, the top half of the church was gone and the remains of the bottom half consisted of about twelve feet in height of jagged wall. The large door at the entrance had fallen flat and as Darren drove over it, the top of his cab scraped against the arch that had once framed it.

The inner door hung off what remained of the frame, it swung loose and by the lights of his digger Darren saw a sight that would have driven normal men to the very edge of their sanity.

What swept erratically side to side behind the door was a mouth, a huge circular maw in which row upon row of teeth appeared to move independently of each other. Great gobs of mucus flew from it as the creature raged in its birthing pain.

Darren lowered his bucket until it touched the floor and drove forward a little to fill it with debris. He then lifted it and assumed the lance-like position that Albert had used.

He opened the cab door. Although the cab offered no protection from this thing should it become aware of him Darren still felt incredibly vulnerable, almost naked as he left it. He jumped down and quickly selected a large brick that he was able to carry.

He heaved the brick into the cab and climbed back inside. Carefully he positioned its heavy weight over his foot, as it in turn hovered over the accelerator. If there was no pressure on the accelerator the vehicle would rapidly come to a halt. A dead man's brake. Darren had no intention of being a dead man.

He waited until there was a lull in the monsters thrashing. He could see that with each passing moment more of the thing was becoming visible, filling the church, its mouth getting closer to actually touching the hanging door. He had to delay it. Between him and Albert they had to make it stay where it was.

They had said that *candles* had weakened the portal and Darren thought that perhaps the things great size was too much for it, the portal was already collapsing and dragging it back into the hell it came from. But still not fast enough. It was winning its struggle, meter by meter it was gaining entry into the world.

Darren hit the accelerator and drove at the mouth. Before the digger passed the doorway he pushed open the cab door and jumped. He hit the rubble strewn floor awkwardly and tumbled. Feeling a bone in his arm snap as the unforgiving bricks broke his fall. He prayed that his carefully balanced rock had dropped onto the accelerator.

It had done its job. The digger ploughed on directly into the creature's mouth. The heavy load in the bucket gave it extra momentum and it raced on into the tooth coated throat. The teeth sliced and cut at the metal as it was hurled inside under its own speed and weight. The creature suddenly lurched, more pronounced than its considerable movements had already been.

Albert's digger was pushed away and almost barrel rolled across the churchyard. The thing coughed and spasmed as it tried to dislodge the metal monster that rested inside it.

The thing then retched and slammed its body up and down onto the ground until finally the digger was forced out of its throat. The machine flew over Darren as he lay dazed on the rubble and crashed into churchyard.

The hellish cry that it had made as it had first begun to emerge sounded again only this time Darren thought it harsher and perhaps more intense. The ground began to vibrate and swell as before. Darren regained his senses, he had to get away from here fast.

The pain from his shoulder caused him to gasp as he stood. He could feel scuffs and scrapes on his legs and face and had to hold his left arm to stop it swinging as the pain was tremendous.

He made for the only light he could see, a single lamp shining from the mangled digger.

Albert had to break the Perspex window of his cab to get out. It was more difficult than he had thought it would be as the plastic bent with his kicks rather than shattering. Finally, a decent crack appeared and instead of kicking at it he pushed his back against the floor and his feet into the centre of the weakened area. It gave.

As he clambered out he saw that the creature was in a state of violent action. It raised its great head, which was almost all mouth, and then slammed it down onto the ground causing the digger and all of the debris around it to lift into the air for a moment. The remains of the church walls finally crumbled and the rest of the monster was revealed.

Albert could see that around what he could only call its middle the pulsing light that had been present earlier had returned. The portal.

Now, instead of emerging from the dimensional gate the creature was being pulled back into it. The forces that had allowed it to seek entry to this world were diminished, and as the Portal began to shrink it was sucking in anything caught in its vortex.

The Chthonian howled and writhed at being denied its escape but couldn't compete with the incredible cosmic force of the gateway as it closed. As it sank further it issued long slathering tentacles from the mouth that grasped at any remaining structure it could find, as though it might prevent it being drawn back to its own world.

But nothing could stop it now. A few seconds later it was gone, and the ground became solid and still once more.

Albert breathed deeply, his body realising that it had stopped doing this for a while.

The unusual atmospherics that had accompanied the summoning dissipated and from behind more typical winter clouds a clear and full moon lit the scene. It revealed complete devastation. The church was nothing more than rubble and splintered supports. The churchyard looked as though it had been stirred by some great spoon, mixing and mashing the gravestones and monuments.

Albert could see that the Abbey, the landmark ruin that had stood for nine hundred years was gone. He supposed that the rest of the land had finally given way and it now rested in the sea.

A voice called to him. It was Norris.

'Albert… Albert!'

Albert turned to see a lofty figure striding quickly towards him in the moonlight, occasionally having to hop over fallen statues and headstones that rested at odd angles.

'I'm alright,' Albert called back to him, 'find Darren, look for him… he went around to the front I think.'

He saw Norris stop and change direction towards where the entrance had once been.

As Norris approached the courtyard, or what had been the courtyard, he saw the figure of Darren sat upon his upturned Digger.

As Norris walked towards him Darren didn't turn his head, but he must have heard him. 'You blokes have got some explaining to do.'

Norris stopped, 'Yes, I suppose we do,' he said, not really sure where the conversation was to go from here, 'how are you, are you hurt?' he asked, to try and keep the subject matter as normal as was allowed given the circumstances.

'Broke my arm I think,' Darren said, he still didn't look at Norris. Instead he gazed at the ruin before him, 'a bit bruised, a bit battered… how about you?'

'I'm alright, I had to take cover when the church… exploded, but I was near to a wall and it kept me covered.'

As he finished his sentence Albert appeared.

'Are you alright', Albert said to Darren, he then turned to Norris, 'Is he alright?' he said this with a tilt of his head indicating that he was actually asking two different questions with the same words.

'He's fine, other than possibly a broken arm he believes, and yes I think he is *fine*.' Norris said with an obvious emphasis on the latter expression.

'I know what you mean you know,' Darren said. He turned to the two friends.

'No one should be able to experience what just happened, to see something like that and not go out of their fucking mind.'

He started to climb down from the cab carefully, still holding his arm. Albert and Norris moved to help him but he shook his head at them. 'No, it's Ok.'

He came to stand by them, so that he could look into their eyes.

'I could feel it at the back of my thoughts, the urge to just drop to the floor and start gibbering like a madman. That thing... it was... wrong, it wasn't just awful, a monster, it wasn't right... *in this place*,' he said.

Norris placed a hand on his shoulder and Darren didn't attempt to shrug it off or move away.

'When things come from other dimensions they have a form that is not only ghastly and alien to us, they have angles to them that human minds simply cannot comprehend.'

'Then how come I'm not blithering, why weren't you and Albert affected,' Darren said.

His face was pained and Norris and Albert could see that the emotions he had held in check were now bubbling to the surface.

'I can't say how you managed to endure it Darren, but I suspect it is the same reason that myself, Albert and Alf...'

Norris paused. Swallowed, and continued, 'The same reason that we are less vulnerable. As you said we have a lot of explaining to do, but in the meantime we also have a lot of work to do to make what has happened here make sense to people.'

'What do you mean?' Darren asked.

Albert took over, 'We can't let anyone know what occurred here Darren, it would be disastrous for everyone if the truth of this was even hinted at.'

'You want to cover it up? How could you possibly cover this up?'

'There are people already on their way to help us. I made a call as soon as we knew the size of what was about to happen, and things are in motion to stop this from becoming anything other than a tragic seismic event,' Norris said.

'A tragic seismic event?'

'Yes. Look, it's best if you leave now. Albert will take you to his place and explain as much as can be explained without you thinking we should be committed.'

Darren lowered his eyes and appeared to be in deep thought over the matter. Norris and Albert waited patiently.

'Alright,' he said after a few moments. 'I'll come, but I need to know everything, whether it makes you look like crazies or not. I just saw some kind of snake people summon a dimensional super-monster so I think that relative to that anything you have to tell me will be kind of mundane.'

Albert stepped forward and slipped his arm around Darren's back to guide him away from the remains of the church. 'I'm sure you're right Darren.' Albert said soothingly, 'I'm sure you're right.'

Albert looked back to Norris who raised his eyebrows.

He was happier to stay here and deal with the clean-up procedure than to spend the rest of the night revealing to Darren that an awfully large amount of what he knew of his world was based as much on fact as the tooth-fairy.

He watched the young man and his oldest friend, his only friend now, walk away from him, and as they did the dull, repeated *whumpf whumpf whumpf* of helicopter blades chopping at the sky could be heard approaching. They couldn't keep doing this. It would break soon. Innsmouth, Crick Street, Winter Falls, Somerside, and now Whitby, incidents of this magnitude couldn't just be obfuscated well enough much longer.

Norris dusted himself down and returned to the men they had rescued from the diggers. They were still unconscious but were not dead, a small mercy. Drugged, not poisoned.

'Crowley and his damned artefacts, what an arsehole the man was.' Norris thought. He needed someone to blame for Alf, and that old lunatic was as good as any.

Authors Comment

I began to write The Whitby Horror shortly after completing my novel Winter Falls. Phillip is of course an escapee from the events that took place there, without referring to it specifically in the text of Whitby I hoped that readers would gather that poor old Phil is a Deep One, in the later stages of his change.

Alf, Albert and Norris were to be part of a larger story but I realised that this was really the end of their time as Guardians of the harbour town and surrounding area, in fact originally I was going to have the whole of Whitby destroyed by the Chthonian, then a few more ideas came my way and what followed was the story you just read. A sequel of sorts to Whitby is definitely on my to-do list.

I hope you approve of The Two Ronnies homage, I couldn't help myself. I was a big fan of the comedy duo when I was young and really wanted to pay tribute to them. I really felt it worked in the story and without upsetting the narrative. As I write this it's just a week after Ronnie Corbett passed away. Another of my heroes has fallen. I suppose I'll have to just write my own.

Eddie Skelson (2016)

THE EMPTY GOD

As he sat on the park bench Bartholomew Grace rubbed his thumb across the small brass plate fixed into the middle of the top strut. Each week, as he waited for his friend Moses to arrive, he gave it a polish. A lick of saliva onto the skin of a time worn thumb was usually enough to wipe away any grime that had gathered.

The bench was old, at least compared to the seating in other areas of the park. If the date stamped into the brass indicated the year it had been placed in its current position, it had been the resting point of visitors since 1967.

He would have been thirty-nine when its iron legs had been secured in concrete. Not a young man then and certainly not now. He had wondered in the past if perhaps there had been a ceremony for it too, but he couldn't tell for whom it would have been held as the rest of the information had been worn away into mere glyphs in the metal.

Bart had chosen this bench to meet, not because of its age, but rather its vantage. It commanded a magnificent view of the lake and was near enough to the edge, which was free of fencing, to scatter seeds and breadcrumbs for the various birds that strutted and waddled across the short grass, and occasional small mammals that bravely scampered across it. The creatures had become accustomed to his visits and many were now confident enough to come within a foot of him, but still wary, casting occasional glances his way as they gobbled down broken biscuits

Bart hoped that Mo wouldn't be late today. It was his last day, and it was important that Mo was here. Mo *had* to see.

'*It is the only way I can make you believe,*' Bart thought.

It would be hard on his friend, terribly hard, but there was no other way, it had to be done. Naturally it would hard for him too, but Bart wouldn't allow fear to distract him. Mo would hear, and then Mo would see and then… well, after that Bart could only hope that his friend would do what had to be done.

It was early, and the park was mostly empty of people. An occasional student walked briskly by. A young woman appeared, pushing a pram from which the chuckles of a baby floated in the air. Mo watched as she leaned her face forward and blew small kisses, to the delight of the little bundle inside. As she neared the bench Bart lifted his hat a little and smiled, receiving a pleasant 'Morning,' in return.

Once she had passed by he checked his watch. Mo should be here soon, any minute. Bart looked along the path which curved around the far side of the lake and past the small, shuttered boathouse that was used to store advertising boards and various safety signs.

The boathouse was the only thing visible in the park, other than the bench he sat upon, that was formed of the rigid and exacting shapes that men created. Everything else was the product of nature making her choices.

Bart had settled his mind that it was there, from the boathouse, it would come for him. It was always the angles that gave it access and the sawed and planed timbers were a construction of such things.

There was no sign of him yet but there were still a few minutes for Mo to be officially late. He could *not* be late today, today of all days, because it was the last day he had.

He continued to gaze across the lake and fixed his attention on the spot where the path met with large gates at the West entrance to the park, deliberately ignoring the boathouse. A moment later, as the woman with the pram was about to the exit the park he saw a figure with the unmistakable stride of Moses Essner entering it.

Bart smiled a little as he observed his friend do as he had done. Mo lifted his hat to the woman as she passed by him, raising his dark fedora a little higher, and offering a larger smile than Bart had presented. Mo then continued along the path.

As his friend approached Bart stood to greet him. Mo beamed once again as he neared and as they met their hands reached out to grip each other in unison.

'Professor!' Moses exclaimed, 'can you believe it's been a week?'

Mo shook Bart's hand vigorously his smile was broad and welcoming. Mo had been a handsome man in his prime and perhaps even more so into his later years. Bart knew that Mo's smile and charm had turned the head of many a lady over the years, and he had also disarmed suspicious husbands and distracted competing suitors with it. Bart was saddened that shortly he might remove that smile forever.

'You know you are not supposed to call me that,' Bart tried to frown as though to admonish Mo, but failed to be convincing, 'but yes Moses, how it flies my friend.'

Bart let his smile take its place and indicated that they should sit.

As Mo sat he wagged a finger disapprovingly at Bart, 'and I wish you would call me Mo, always its Moses with you, only my mother, *both of them*,' he exclaimed, 'ever called me Moses.'

'Your mother had standards Moses.' Both men laughed, they had indulged in ridiculous and pleasant jibes towards each other for many years. Mo removed his hat and placed it next to him and took a look out across the lake.

Each week in foul or fine weather the two met at this same spot. When the season blessed them with the sun, or at least an absence of rain they sat on the bench and chatted for a few hours. The topics were invariably politics, history, sport and occasionally Mo's still surprisingly varied love life, after which they would make their way to a café situated near the park which served homemade pies and pastries.

When the weather was against them they would make directly for the café. Mo was especially prone to feeling the bite of cold weather of late, and so when winter brought ice and sleet they would meet there almost every week and forgo the bench. Today there was only a very light breeze. July had been a good month so far, bringing hot days and warm nights.

'No ducks,' Mo said.

'No, at least I've not seen any since I arrived,' Bart replied.

'Ah, well I have some sunflower seeds and bread,' Mo reached into a pocket and withdrew a Sunblest Loaf bag that was half full of crusts and seeds, 'let's see if they come out for breakfast'.

'You spoil those creatures you know; you probably do them more harm than good with all that,' Bart indicated the weighty bag.

'Nonsense Bart, it's a treat for them. And besides, I never know how many there will be. I don't like the little ones to miss out.'

Mo began to toss portions of bread and seed toward the lakes edge. Bart thought that this revealed the nature of his friend in a nutshell. Always a considerate man and always prepared to provide for others, especially the young, especially the weak. He checked his watch, which was noticed by Mo.

'Appointment?' he asked.

'No… well, yes I do have an appointment,' Bart replied. There was silence for a moment. Mo expected his friend to elaborate but he simply stared out at the lake, clearly turning something over in his mind.

Mo frowned. It wasn't hard to spot when something was troubling Bart. The tell-tale turn of his mouth, the way he would stare off into space. They knew each other well after all as their friendship had begun over fifty years ago. Both men were of German Jewish birth and had the misfortunate to have been born in a time and place time when being Jewish was practically a curse.

Mo had been lucky enough to be sent away to stay with friends in France, as Hitler rose to power using his message of hate for the Jewish race. His parents had not been so fortunate.

Determined to 'ride out the storm' his father had tried to maintain his business in Berlin, but had been forcibly closed down by the Nazi's. Shortly after that, as they too attempted to leave for France, they had been arrested on a charge of 'conspiracy,' but conspiracy to do what had never been determined. Soon after they had both been sent to work camps and that was the last anyone ever heard of them.

It was only through further good fortune that Mo had again been moved on to friends, this time in Britain. Just a week later Hitler's Blitzkrieg struck France. As a child he had watched the whole of the war unfold only in newspapers, as he lived in luxury with wealthy relatives in the Welsh countryside.

Bart had not escaped the Nazi's.

On his forearm he bore the tell-tale number that designated him as a concentration camp prisoner. The two had met after the war had finally finished claiming the lives of their families and friends. Moses had returned to Berlin to study, funded by his new family, and it was there that he had quickly formed a friendship with the enigmatic Bartholomew Grace, one of the few survivors of the Treblinka death camp.

Bart had never discussed his time in the camp and Mo had never felt comfortable asking about it. In truth he harboured a mild, but ever present guilt, that he had been so fortunate where others had suffered so greatly.

Only once did he directly confess this to Bart who had brushed it off with an incredible lack of concern. He uttered only a single statement regarding the issue, which had puzzled Mo completely.

'I have experienced much worse than the Holocaust,' he had said dismissively, and that had ended all present and future conversation about it.

'Should we head to the Café now?' Mo asked, 'if you have an appointment?'

Bart licked his lips and seemed not to hear at first but then turned and looked intently at his friend. It unnerved Mo a little. Bart had striking blue eyes that had no tint of age about them and when they focused on something, or someone, Bart fancied that laser beams might shoot from them.

When they were focused on *him* he found it difficult to blink and his eyes grew watery from the breeze. It was like being caught in the gaze of a basilisk.

'Moses, I must tell you something today, and I know it will sound strange and almost certainly make you doubt my sanity. but will you hear me out?'

Whatever he had expected Bart to say this was not at all close to it. Mo struggled to reply at first as he digested the words but finally found his voice, and answered a little apprehensively.

'Of course Bart. *Whatever* you have to say I'll listen,' Moses dug into himself and found some humour, 'You're not getting married are you?'

He gave a short nervous laugh and beamed his broad smile, but Bart didn't return it.

'Moses, my friend, what I have to say is by any measure shocking, and you will not believe a word of it, trust me. No matter how long we have been friends and our respect for each other you will not believe it,' his expression was grave and vaguely sympathetic.

Moses was a taken aback that Bart might not believe or trust him, a little resolve crept back into his voice.

'Say what you have to say Bart, I think it is only fair that your judgement of me should at least wait until I have heard your words.'

Bart nodded, his lips were tightly sealed, 'so be it' they said without words.

'Do you know what Judaism is Moses, and by that I mean why it was different from all of the religions that were abundant at the time, when it came to be?'

Mo frowned, for a moment unsure of what the question meant or how to answer it, 'Um, ...it was the first of the great monotheistic religions?' Moses asked, rather than told. He felt like he was being given a test at school.

'Exactly right my friend, exactly right,' Bart gave a Mo a reassuring smile, 'I will not embarrass myself by asking if you know the history of the Torah, because you are as well versed as anyone I know, but do you know much of what came before it?'

Mo relaxed a little. Bart was a Professor of languages and the history of language. While he had chosen to study business and finance, a world of numbers, his friend had lost himself in the world of letters. Bart spoke at least eight languages fluently, that he knew of, including Japanese and various forms of Arabic, but Bart's speciality, the thing that had earned him his Professorship, was the study of 'dead languages,' those of the Incans, the Mayans, Celts and Saxons.

They had lost touch for many years as Bart had disappeared on trips to cities that had been buried and forgotten. It was a fact that it was only in the last three years that Bart had settled and they had begun their regular meetings at the bench.

'I'm not sure that I do Bart,' Mo replied, 'this is your thing I suppose'

'Yes, it is, or it is at least something I have found myself drawn too over the years,'

Bart gave a slight nod.

'Unfortunately Mo my interest, my curiosity, has taken me to places that I wish I had never been and I have witnessed things that I truly wish I had never seen and that they had not seen me.'

Before Mo could ask what he meant Bart continued,

'Abraham took the word of the one true God to his people, and they moved across the land, guided by him. This of course you know.'

Mo didn't lose his frown but acknowledged the fact.

'Before this the people were beholden to many Gods. They worshipped and prayed to demons, djinn's and other entities they believed would grant them great gifts and powers. These were beings that would also punish them if they did not offer sacrifices and suffer total obedience. For thousands of years Moses, mankind lived in the shadow of these Gods, slaves to them and their vile corruption, until finally Abraham came along and saved us all,' Bart fixed Mo with his hypnotic blue eyes, 'Does that make sense to you Bart?'

'Yes I suppose so,' Bart replied, 'it's hard to argue with the logic at least.'

'Good. Then let me ask you my friend, what do you think happened to the other Gods?'

'I'm sorry?' Mo asked.

'Gods, that have been around for... let's say a thousand years, suddenly they are gone. What do you think happened to them?'

'What do you mean *happened to them*, they didn't exist, nothing happened to them. People just stopped believing in them.' Bart said, perplexed.

'But this new God Moses, the *one* God did, it did exist?'

'What?' Bart shook his head a little, 'I'm not sure I get what you are driving at?'

'Moses, you are telling me that you believe that our ancestors believed, for a long time, in a variety of Gods, but then stopped doing so because a new God came along, yes or no?'

'Well yes, of course, but Bart, this is not just *some God*. It is the creator, the one God who created us, revealing himself to save mankind. What is this Bart? Are you telling me you are now an atheist?'

Bart shook his head, 'Far, far from it Moses. I can promise you that I wholeheartedly believe that Gods are real. However, I'm afraid ours isn't.'

Moses felt his jaw go slack, 'Is this a joke?' he said, but Bart continued.

'The Old Gods that our ancestors worshipped were real, very real. They slaughtered us, used us for unspeakable practices for which I cannot even begin to explain in the short time I have. They used us to fight their wars and they fed on us, we were literally food for the Gods Bart. The only way to end this was to bring hope to our species, to stop them from worshipping these creatures and by doing so reduce their power. The things that have happened to us recently, the *magic* that everybody is talking about, this is the force that we have and that they want.'

Mo felt that he should stop Bart from continuing, this was the kind of talk he heard in the supermarkets and coffee shops all the time of late. The news had been awash with reports of claims that the supernatural had finally been proven, that 'magic' was real.

It had been building up for a while, internet blogs, YouTube, Twitter had been rife with people claiming to have evidence of everything from psychic ability to demonic possession.

Then the dam had broken. An announcement from the recently installed Prime Minister, after a tragic accident had claimed both the party leader and his deputy, had brought the business to a head.

'Magic is real,' he had said. The phrase was the headline of every newspaper in the world. Except America, it was noted.

Surely this had affected his friend a little. Perhaps he was going through a crisis of his faith due to the terrible pressure the news had put upon all religions. Mo didn't interrupt, instead he listened carefully for an indication that Bart was either pulling his leg or in some kind of depression.

'We are the conduits,' Bart continued, 'and we feed our force directly to them when we throw ourselves at their mercy.'

Bart leaned in, he raised his hands as though holding an invisible ball.

'Abraham created a *new* God to fear and obey, to worship. He had power himself Bart, Abraham was able to channel this *force*, this *Essence* as they are calling it now, he could manipulate its energies so well that he was able to perform what would appear to be miracles, granted by his God. He convinced those around him that he was a prophet and an emissary of this new deity, and slowly, upon seeing his power, people began to turn away from the Great Old Ones. By getting his people to pray to the empty God, Abraham *stole power* from the Old Ones and weakened their hold over us,' Bart paused.

Moses scrutinised his friend. Bart was good-humoured almost always, but not *whacky*, he wasn't one for practical jokes or pranks.

Moses tried to muster some kind of retort or at least a few words to bring the conversation back to safe ground but Bart's conviction and his laser eyes held him firmly.

'Moses I am telling you this because there are things that I need you to do as I'm afraid I cannot do them. I will not be around after today, at least not as you know it.'

At this Mo finally tried to speak but Bart held up his hands to stop him.

'Something is coming for me, in fact it is almost here, and it is going to kill me...'

Finally, unable to process any more of Bart's nonsense, Moses cut his friend short.

'Oh for God's sake Bart, what the hell are you gibbering about?' Moses spluttered the words, but Bart continued, talking over Mo's pleas that he stop.

'Moses I have been to places that can only be reached by certain means, certain rituals have to be performed. I have been to places outside of the dimension we occupy, to ones with beautiful, and *terrible* creatures existing within them. Moses, there is a creature hunting me. Once it saw me I was doomed, from that very moment on and this thing *will not stop*. In these places there are laws and rules, just as there are here, but they are often different Bart, strange, defying what we think of as logic. If a Tiger spotted you, it might hunt you until you left its territory, to keep its right to its domain, perhaps this thing *fears* those that see it, and hunts them to oblivion, none can say, but I assure you it would hunt me until the end of time if that's how long took took. I have kept it away with sigils and rituals but these break and become less potent over time. I have only one recourse left open to me, which may not work in the manner I hope for, I know of a man who achieved what I propose to attempt, and it may fail, but it *will prove* to you that I am *not* insane.' Bart looked beyond him, to the boathouse Mo thought.

'It is almost here, but you will not be able see it, for which I am eternally thankful. This thing is not visible to us in this dimension, only in its own. You *will* see what it does however, and for that I am truly sorry my friend.'

Bart took a slight pause but then continued to prevent Moses from talking.

'In my home I have hidden some books and my notes. The books are old and they are dangerous, you cannot read them by normal means, but don't take the risk of trying. My notes are written in my own cipher. There is a Professor at Harvard who has the key to it. You will need to speak to him, but do it discreetly, there is something going on in the US that doesn't seem right. I've posted some items to you and you are the sole beneficiary of my Will, my assets are substantial.'

Bart stopped.

Moses realised that he still gripped the Sunblest Loaf bag tightly and it had swelled like a balloon, almost to the point of popping, but he paid it no attention.

Mo took a breath and then spoke calmly, 'Let me recap if I may. You are saying that *my* God doesn't exist, but that other Gods do. That they feed off this *Essence* thing that all of the papers and the television people are talking about, and so the prophet Abraham, who wasn't really a prophet, invented *The* God so that mankind would be… weaned off the others, the older, bad Gods. You have been to other dimensions, though you have not clearly explained how that came about, and because of that there is a monster that followed you, and is going to kill you, oh… and it won't stop until it kills you. Finally, when it does, I get your notes, some magical books and all your money. How am I doing?'

Moses was surprised as Bart smiled at him, more warmly, and sympathetically than he had ever done in the past.

'Actually Moses, I think you have it all perfectly.'

Bart reached out and closed his hands around the Mo's hand that clutched the duck food.

'You have been a good friend all these years and I'm sorry that I have to leave you with this. But I trust you Moses, I trust you and I *believe* in you.'

Bart released the Mo's hand and stood. He looked at his watch.

'Almost time,' he said, 'the ritual will break soon.'

He moved away from the bench and towards the edge of the lake. For a moment Moses thought that perhaps Bart might intend to drown himself, but then checked this. The lake was five feet in depth at most, no more than two at the edge.

'Look Bart, shall we just go to the Café, you can tell me…'

Moses stopped talking as his ears popped. It was as though he had just taken a sudden drop in altitude. The space around Bart seemed to warp in and out for a second and a smell like burning electrical wire reached his nose.

Bart was stood at the edge of the lake and he had closed his eyes. He was mouthing words quietly to himself. Was he praying? Moses thought he wasn't, something told him that these were not the words of *his* scripture or of any holy book he knew of.

In a heartbeat Bart's body appeared to explode in all directions at once, as if invisible blades had sliced through him from all angles. Chunks of him flew into the air and a mist of blood formed a red cloud where he had stood. In a moment, pieces of flesh and blood-soaked cloth rained down onto the ground and splashed into the lake.

Moses dropped the bag of seeds and bread to the floor. He stared at the remains of his friend as they bobbed in the water and oozed on the grass. He dropped to his knees and clasped his hands together.

'Oh my God, oh my God,' he screamed to no one.

CREECE

Part One

London, 2045

'John Creece, Metropolitan police,' he said, flashing a badge to the eye-scan unit to the left of the doorframe. A red dot in its centre winked as it registered the information. In an instant a monitor on the other side of the door brought up his details and image (as provisioned by the England and Wales Personal Information Act of 2025). The old lady on the other side of the door squinted at the picture and compared it to what she could see of the man in the camera.

The digital snapshot framed a **sombre** looking man in his early thirties with mousey brown hair and dark eyes. The man behind the door looked equally moody, had the same brown hair and from what she could tell as she zoomed the camera into his face, the same deep brown eyes. He appeared a little older than the computerised version, perhaps another ten years had passed since this picture had been snapped but he appeared far healthier in person than the over exposed representation on her view screen.

'How can I help you Officer?' she asked through the intercom.

'Ah…You called us ma'am… about the cats?'

There was a moment's silence from the speaker then a crackle. Abruptly the heavy '*clunk*' of a locking mechanism resonated down the hall and the jingle-jangle of a chain followed. Creece smiled, it amused him that even with the high security protocols and installations these apartments were fitted with so many of the older generation still trusted in the strength of few links of chain to protect them from the evils of the world.

As the door opened fully he gave the old lady, traditional blue rinse and large glasses, a well-trained smile of thanks as she invited him in.

'You know I didn't think anybody was going to come, I called three days ago,' the old lady said as she walked slowly ahead.

'It can take a while for these things to come to my desk Ms Stack,' Creece replied.

She led him to a living room and indicated that he should sit in a large armchair which was currently occupied by a very large ginger cat.

'Samson, shoo!' She waved the cat off the chair and it skulked out of the room.

'Would you like me to take your coat Officer?'

Although the weather was mild when he had left the office Chris Darlington, the sixty-eight year old Department Chief had advised him that it would rain within the next few hours so he had donned his Macintosh. When it came to predicting the weather no one in the office failed to listen to Chris, he once told Creece that he could feel the weight of a cloud and smell a Saharan wind pushing against an Atlantic breeze.

His accurate record spoke for itself and Creece had no doubt that when he left this building the rain would be pouring where it had previously been a warm, dry summer day.

'No thank you Ms Stack I'll be fine,' he said, sitting.

His frame, large and muscular was an issue with furnishings made for more average sized people and he found himself resting on the very edge of the seat. A mild subconscious fear of becoming wedged between the armrests and then standing up with a chair attached to his backside briefly entered his thoughts.

He took a quick look around the room. Sometimes it was difficult to get people to talk in a relaxed way, however, by noticing some family photo or heirloom on a shelf he could usually engage them in general chat and bring them into his confidence. A happy and comfortable person revealed a lot more information than a nervous and guarded one. Interrogation Handbook - Rule 101.

The apartment was typical of its design, a long hall off which were four rooms, two bedrooms, a bathroom and larger room at the end that was split into a small kitchen area and living room. The décor of the house was very old fashioned, being a mix of styles from the twentieth century. Only the Holo-Media centre fixed into the wall was evidence of any real twenty first century technology.

Ms Stack sat almost opposite him in a similar chair to his although this one had two small cushions upon which were embroidered little cats in various action poses. Looking around the room revealed various cat pictures, figures, trophies and other feline miscellany. Twenty years of detective work told him that the lady liked cats.

He suppressed a smirk that was building up from amusement at his self-depreciation and the absurdity of him being sent out to investigate this call and focused on the job at hand.

'Would you like a cup of tea Officer?' Ms Stack enquired.

'No thank you, had a cup just a short while ago,' he said, pulling out a notebook, 'If you could just tell me what you told my colleague when you telephoned...I have some notes here but I would appreciate it first-hand'

Ms Stack sat with her hands clasped on her lap. She looked reasonably relaxed and Creece always tried to interview people in their own home for this very reason.

'Well, about two weeks ago one of my little ones passed away,' she started

'One of your cats?'

'Yes, my Elizabeth. She had been ill for some time, of course she was so very old.'

Creece nodded and scribbled '*Dead Moggy*' on his notepad.

'So I wrapped her in her favourite blanket and put her into one of the boxes that my shopping arrives in. I'm afraid I can't walk very far Officer and even a light box with my poor Elizabeth in it would cause my back to act up.'

Creece nodded again but said nothing to allow her to continue.

'Well, Elizabeth passed away on the Tuesday and my helper, Jasmine, wouldn't be over until Wednesday. Unless I call of course, but I do hate to be a bother.' Ms Stack shook her head a little.

Creece continued to nod in an understanding way. He also noted the date for Tuesday, two weeks ago. Ms Stack waited patiently as he scribbled.

'Please continue Ms Stack and do call me John, my name is John Creece.'

'Oh, thank you,' Ms Stack replied and smiled. 'Well you must call me Alice, Officer Creece.'

His practiced smile reappeared in acknowledgment and he decided not to pursue the informal path.

'Now, where was I?' Alice thought for a moment, 'ah yes,

Tuesday. Well, I went to bed at about ten thirty, that's my normal bed time Officer Creece.'

She paused to give him time to write down this piece of information, which she clearly considered salient. Creece dutifully made a note of this though it was mostly to encourage the old lady to continue giving him details, no matter how small. This was another valuable lesson from his mental 'Book of Interrogation,' never appear to disregard or belittle information from the interviewee.

'I was awoken at four am by one of my little darlings crying Officer Creece and I was quite curious about this because I am very rarely wakened by any of their calls or antics while I'm asleep.'

Alice leaned in towards Creece, turning her heard slightly.

Creece mimicked her movement. A matter of secrecy or something 'unusual' was about to be shared.

'I looked around the apartment to see which of them was crying but they were all *fast asleep,*' Alice lowered her voice a little, a conspirational whisper between her and Creece, 'then I heard scratching coming from the hallway. I thought it might be one of the cats that lives further down the hall. Perhaps it had sneaked in through the doorway without my noticing it.'

She moved her head a little closer in and again Creece followed suit.

'I turned on the hall light but there was *nothing,* but then I heard the scratching again Officer, and the crying.'

She paused, for effect Creece was certain.

'The sounds were coming from *Elizabeth's box!*'

Ms Stack placed her hands flat on her knees and returned to an upright position with an expression that asked 'what do you think about that!'

Creece also sat straight and tried to project a similar air of amazement despite not really understanding what was amazing.

'I opened up the box and there was Elizabeth, mewing and pawing at the sides!'

Creece made a point of not scribbling now, Alice was clearly reaching the finale, he simply waited for the final revelation that would hopefully underline why he was sitting here listening to a story about cats.

'Officer Creece I was *astounded,*' she gasped the end of the sentence as if she were telling this to an audience of little children, 'I was absolutely certain that Elizabeth had passed away, but *there* she was!'

Alice waited, to let the startling news to sink in.

Creece leaned back a little. He didn't want to frown as it might upset the old lady but he wasn't a hundred percent certain that all of her dogs were barking. It was par for the course that he had to attend any number of bogus or hoax calls and he was glad that he had patience to at least see them through to the end of the tale. After all, he had been 'fixed up' many times before, *but* he had to temper that thought with the fact that he had been proven wrong on more than one of those occasions too.

'So if I understand you correctly Ms Stack, um...Alice. Elizabeth died of natural causes on Tuesday, but in the early hours of the next morning, she was alive and well.'

'Yes that's correct Officer,' Alice agreed.

'Therefore, you believe that there may be paranormal involvement?' he cautiously.

'Yes, and I informed the police. Immediately. I saw on the news about reporting instances of the dead being seen walking, so I called the local police station and they said that I should give my statement to one of your colleagues in the DPI?'

Creece took a breath. The good old local Bobbies had struck again. Can't be bothered to fill out the paperwork? Send it to the DPI. Confused old ladies? Send them to the DPI.

'Yes, it stands for the Department for Paranormal Investigation Alice,' he said wearily.

Alice was deadly earnest though. Whatever this 'situation' was *she* clearly felt that it was important and who was he to take lightly what someone who was obviously polite, educated and sensitive thought might require investigation? Still, this was taking up time and time was a commodity he could not afford to squander. He had to wrap it up, show some interest in the errant moggy perhaps, thank the old dear for her vigilance and community spirit, stroke one of the cats and leave.

'Alice, perhaps could I take a look at Elizabeth is she here at the moment?' he asked as he rose from the chair.

'Oh no, I'm afraid not Officer Creece, she's dead.'

Creece paused for a beat, 'dead *again* Alice?'

'Yes I'm afraid so, the poor darling. You see when Jasmine

came over on Wednesday she let the cats out for their walk. They like to venture out down the fire escape and into the alley, *that* window is never closed Officer Creece, not very secure at all,' Alice frowned.

'Elizabeth followed the others outside and I asked Jasmine to keep an eye on her, you know, because of her funny turn the day before. The next thing I know Jasmine comes running in, face a picture, and says that Elizabeth just been run over by a car!' Alice shook her head but continued.

'Well, the poor girl was awfully upset but I told her not to worry. She said that Elizabeth had made her way down the fire escape and then just dashed into the road. She ran straight into all that traffic. It's a very busy road Officer Creece and they drive much too fast on there,' Alice shook her head in admonishment.

'One of the neighbours from the ground floor took care of her. Mr Gerard, he's a lovely man, he used to be in banking. He said it would be better if I remembered how Elizabeth was *before* as the accident had been *very nasty.*'

Alice's voice strained a little at this. Creece could see that losing her companion for what appeared to be a second time had been quite hard on her. However, it was looking like his trip had indeed been a waste of time.

'Well, I'm very sorry that you had to endure such a loss twice Alice,' he presented her with his best look of commiseration, 'but I'm afraid that there's not really a great deal I can do if Elizabeth is no longer with...'

'Oh but I didn't call because of *Elizabeth* Officer Creece,' Alice interrupted, 'no not at all! I called because she was the *second* one I had seen rise from the dead,' she pursed her lips.

'You mean this has happened to one of your cats before?' Creece asked cautiously.

'No Officer Creece! Really, do you honestly think I would waste police time over one of my pets,' she frowned at him, 'I have seen a dead *person.*'

Creece opened his notebook and sat back down.

'I'm listening,' he said.

Part Two

Creece rapped on the door, solid knocks that echoed down the corridor but which would barely be heard in the apartment due to the effective soundproofing that all of the units had. Of course there was a doorbell and the intercom system, but Creece thought that the shrill ring of a bell didn't convey the authority of a good firm knock, it was 'Presenting Authority 101.'

After listening to the old lady's story once again he informed the office and ordered a full containment team to the scene. He knew that his best course of action now was to wait patiently for them to arrive. He should secure the building and investigate Ms Stack's story with maximum back up. His patience had lasted approximately three minutes.

Alice had told him that the gentleman across the hall, a Mr Beresford (who worked as an accountant and was very respectable, always smartly dressed), had recently suffered the loss of his son David, who was only seventeen years old, to bowel cancer and this only three years since his wife had died of a similar condition

She had remarked upon how Mr Beresford, on the rare occasion that she saw him, had plainly sunk into a deep depression.

'He looked like a man haunted Officer Creece,' she had said.

Alice then explained that on the evening that Elizabeth had passed away she had seen Mr Beresford entering his apartment with another man and that when she had said hello to him he had bustled the stranger into his home and slammed the door shut.

'How odd for Mr Beresford to be so rude I thought, he is usually so nice.' Alice said.

A few days later she had gone to visit Mr Gerard with a pot-roast she had cooked by way of thanks for him taking care of Elizabeth after the accident in the road and that it was on her return from that visit that she saw the dead person.

'As plain as day Mr Beresford's son was *walking down the corridor!*' Alice had tilted her head sideways a little and pulled a strange face, which Creece assumed was her interpretation of how the walking dead looked. Or she was having a stroke.

He rapped once again on the door and a little more forcefully this time. He *knew* that there was someone behind it. Right now this person was looking at him via the closed circuit TV monitor, he could *feel* the fear that was building up behind the inch-thick reinforced door that stood between him and the occupier. Everyone had their abilities these days, or at least almost everyone. Most were mild expressions of what had come to be known as the paranormal, inconsequential in effect or at least no more than a quirk of an individual.

It was rude to ask a person's ability. Everyone wanted to of course, even he had to admit that he had been desperate to know if Ms Alice Stack had some amazing supernatural talent, nothing had shown on her file, but you couldn't just ask in a civilised conversation. Sometimes it was infuriating perpetuating the ideal of British reserve and politeness. Very few knew his talent. No one knew the full extent of what he could do. Creece kept this locked away even from his colleagues

It was obvious that the only way this door was going to open for him was if he opened it himself. Decision made he gathered his energy. His eyes fluttered shut as he focused his thoughts. He placed the palm of his hand upon the locking mechanism, let the flood of energy he had accumulated in those few moments coalesce and then released it. In an instant a door that was built to contain raging fires, reduce the sound of an explosion to a whisper and take the impact of a dozen sledgehammers striking in unison, flew open as if an express train had hit it. The locking mechanism shattered into a dozen pieces and scattered onto the floor along with splinters of wood and metal from the frame into the apartments narrow corridor

Creece stepped in.

A middle aged man lay on the floor moaning and holding his head. The door had caught him as he had stepped back from it, which Creece had anticipated, but considered that if the threat inside was real the chance of injury was justified. He glanced down the hall then moved towards the prostrate man and crouched by his side.

'Mr Beresford?' he asked but without force or accusation.

The man continued to hold his hands to his head and groaned in pain. Blood was pouring over his fingers. Creece placed his hands upon those of the injured man and once again focused his energies. This time he didn't summon destruction, instead he allowed a steady flow of controlled energy to pass through him and into the injured man, it cleaned and bonded, it was a healing force.

Beresford felt a wave of calm wash over him. When it had exploded the edge of the door had slammed into his head and a bolt of pain had struck at him like lightning. The impact had left a deep cut near the corner of his eye which pumped blood furiously and his body had begun to go into shock.

However, the pain lifted almost instantly as he felt Creece's large hands cover his own. The sensation was that of a mild, not unpleasant tingle and it spread across his whole body relaxing, his spasming muscles eased and became still. For a brief moment after the contact Mr Beresford felt something that had eluded him for many years now, total calm.

Now, with the pain gone his fear quickly returned and stark panic followed. With a sudden movement and strength borne of fear he pushed Creece away and scrambled on all fours down the hall. Creece stood and made just two long strides to catch up with him, caught his shirt collar, hauled him backwards and lifted the blood soaked accountant to his feet. He pushed Beresford against the wall and pinned him easily to it with just one hand on his chest.

Beresford had never considered himself a strong man by any stretch of the imagination but he couldn't believe the power of the man than stood in front of him. Even with the added surge of adrenalin coursing through his system he couldn't summon strength sufficient enough to do more than helplessly squirm against the hand that kept him locked against the wall. He couldn't even drop to his knees, which was all he felt was worth doing. This man, this policeman, was physically holding his entire body upright with one hand.

Creece examined the terrified man before him. His fear was not simply because the police had just burst into his home. This wasn't a man who had stolen from his employer or abused some privilege. There was something deeper inside him, something both shameful and desperate. He looked for more signs of injury to Beresford but was satisfied that there was no longer any cut beneath the coagulating blood that covered his head and no further injury to the man.

'Mr Beresford?' he asked once again.

Beresford finally began to lose his tension, his body slumped but was still pinned by Creece. He nodded his head.

'Mr Beresford my name is Detective John Creece. I'm from

the Department of Paranormal Investigation...do you understand me?'

'Yes...yes,' tears were streaming down Beresford's face and he croaked out his words between sobs. 'Have you come for...my boy?'

Creece could feel that the panic and the strength that came with it was now drained from this man, he removed his hand and Beresford slowly slid down the wall bringing his hands back to his face. He began to cry and sobbed loudly.

As Beresford sank Creece immediately sensed that he was being watched. He looked to the far end of the hall. A youth in his teens with a mop of dark hair stood with drooped shoulders. He stared at Creece without fear, anger, malevolence or interest.

'He's empty,' was the first thought that came to Creece. He looked down at Beresford who continued to sob into his hands and mutter incomprehensible words. He wasn't going anywhere. He turned his attention back to the youth.

'David Beresford?' he asked and moved cautiously towards him.

The youth made no attempt to move but switched his gaze from Creece to the distraught man on the floor.

'Something missing,' said the youth.

Creece halted. '*Empty*' a voice in his head said to him. He knew was his own conscious thought but it seemed to come from somewhere just beyond his own mind.

'What is missing, David? Creece asked.

The youth continued to look down to the crying man.

'I am,' the boy's voice was flat and held no emotion

Creece waited for a moment to see if the youth, the *dead* David Beresford, would elaborate. Instead he continued to stare with glazed eyes.

'David what happened to you, can you tell me that?' he moved a little closer as he spoke and this time David shifted his gaze back towards him.

'I died,' he said, once again with an eerie flatness.

Creece came to within a few feet of him. He took in the boy's appearance. His clothes all looked new, a shirt with a crisp collar, jeans that showed no sign of fading or fray and trainers with gleaming toecaps instead of the scuffs that are earned from active use. He had thick brown hair with a fringe that dropped just above his eyes, typical of the trend amongst lads his age. But amidst all these outward signs of the living world there were two eyes sunk into a pallid and sagging face that revealed the void that they were socketed into. Despite the fact that David could walk and talk, even communicate, Creece could see that he was undeniably dead.

'Can you tell me how you came to be here David, back in this world?' Creece, edged slightly closer.

David blinked. Automatic. A memory. There was no reply.

'Would you mind if I took your hand David?' Creece asked and stretched out his own palm upwards.

David appeared almost to frown for a moment, he glanced briefly down the corridor at his father, who was lost in his anguish, and then slowly placed his slim hand onto the Detectives.

Creece felt the boy's smooth skin contact his. It wasn't cold or clammy, nor did it spark any instinctive revulsion, but it was a *cool* sensation. The contact allowed Creece to send a pulse of his energy into the boy who shuddered slightly but didn't move his hand away. Creece saw *into* him and through his power he could see what it was that was missing.

He withdrew his hand slowly and David's arm dropped to his side. Creece felt a surge of sadness wash over him, for the father as well as the boy. If there was one sliver of good in all of this, it was that David was not possessed or carrying the plague.

He heard the sound of heavy boots moving up the hall, silent to most but easily detected by himself. The boy's misery would end soon. The fathers would not. He had seen similar situations like this and it wasn't hard figure the story out in this case.

The father, already wracked with grief over the loss of his beloved spouse had channelled all of his heart into his only child only to find that soon fate would also take him too. In desperation and perhaps defiance he had sought out a Necromancer. There were many ways to elicit their help, the Internet was most likely or perhaps some 'friend' who had a friend, who had a friend. Despite the heavy penalties and warnings from the government Beresford had employed one of these shameless bastards to bring his son back from the dead. Of course the powers of these Necromancers varied, the weakest might bring back a walking cadaver that rotted before your eyes and ravenous for flesh. They were undead things which carried an incredibly communicable virus in their bite, turning those they assaulted into equally vile and hellish creatures. These creatures made the Black Death look like a cold sore.

There had also been many instances where a returning soul had brought back *more* than just the dearly departed as well. Whilst he had yet to see such a thing with his own eyes there were reports of possessions and actual manifestations of unearthly beings and creatures that had somehow been caught up in the Necromancers summoning. Perhaps they were even *waiting* for such an opportunity. It was a sobering thought.

In this instance the Necromancer had been certainly been weak or at the very least, sloppy. He had summoned the boy's soul but had not controlled the ritual sufficiently, causing an overlap around the boy's body. So badly controlled in fact that the summoning had spread into the area around the apartment catching poor old Alice's cat in its effect.

Whether the cat had committed suicide he couldn't be sure. He was certain that animals acted upon instincts far better in tune with the paranormal than humans but an act of feline suicide was one for the philosophy boys to consider.

What the Necromancer had left behind was not really David but nor was his former body infested with demons. Instead there was a shell of the boy. It could move and talk but had no will or emotion. It was not evil but then neither was it good. It only existed. As David had said to him, 'something was missing.'

The familiar sound of assault rifles being swung into shoulders caught Creece's attention alerting him that the back-up was here.

He turned, slowly, towards the door and was faced by three men sporting combat armour and in assault formation. They were locked and loaded.

'Detective is everything ok?' the nearest figure calmly called out. He was crouched and his rifle pointed straight at Creece's chest. The trigger was being squeezed with enough pressure to make it happen in a heartbeat. Creece was fast, but not bullet fast.

'Everything is under control,' Creece replied.

He lifted his hands carefully, placed them behind his head and eased down to his knees. The squad moved in cautiously, using tactics tried, tested and honed to perfection. Two men moved past

Creece quickly but with caution while others maintained their aim upon the detective.

Within seconds Beresford was lifted to his feet and cuffed. He was then bustled out still shaking with tears. Creece watched the scene unfold from his knees as more armed men appeared to replace those that had left with Beresford and in turn they joined the men that covered both himself and David with an assortment of firearms.

Finally, Creece saw another figure appear at the doorway. He wore a long coat similar to his and he noticed that the shoulders had damp patches.

'*Raining,*' he thought.

The armed police moved aside as the man made his way down the hall.

'Good afternoon John, couldn't wait eh?' Darlington said

'Afternoon,' Creece replied, looking up. 'You know me Chris, I hate it when cats meet untimely deaths.'

With obvious effort Darlington lowered himself to his knees, he was tempted to state that he was 'getting too old for all of this,' but decided against it. He looked directly into his colleague's eyes. Creece felt Darlington's energy pulse in and around him. He was being investigated, just as he had investigated David Beresford.

'The boy is harmless. A case of bad Necromancy,' Creece said as his body tingled with Darlington's wash of power.

'Anyone killed? Injured?' Darlington asked, seemingly able to do what he did as though he was merely multi-tasking on a computer.

'Just the cat,' Creece replied, surprised that he felt a little sad at that thought.

The old man offered a slight smile and got back to his feet.

'He's fine, carry on,' he said, gesturing to the assault team that they should move on to David.

They moved swiftly past the Detectives and took hold of the boy, who offered no resistance as they quickly bound his hands and feet. Within moments they were moving past Creece with the unresisting youth as the others had with his father.

Once they were gone more armed men moved into the apartment and began to search it. Creece got to his feet.

'We have to find this Necromancer,' Darlington said as he walked Creece out of the apartment, 'this is your top priority now.'

'I know,' Creece replied.

They exited the building in silence. Scores of uniformed police surrounded the building, all armed. Rain was pouring across the city and Creece lifted his collar to ward against it.

'Told you it would rain,' Darlington said.

'Yes you did, yes you did.' Creece replied. A thought occurred to him, and he turned to Chris, working hard to keep a smirk off his lips.

'You know what, I know of a lady in this block that might be looking for a hot date. Could be interested in a mature, official sort like yourself.'

'Oh?' Darlington said and narrowed his eyes at Creece.

'Yeah really, her names Alice, want me to get her number for you?'

'What is she? Some crazy old cat lady?'

'Psychics,' Creece shook his head, 'you suck the joy out of everything.'

THE DEVIL'S ROAD

London, 1745

'Black' Paul Burnip wondered if anyone at all was going to be coming his way this morning, given that he had lain in wait for three hours already and not a soul had moved along the road. He was cold and although it wasn't raining it was damp. A thick mist rolled around the heath soaking his cloak and the moisture was being absorbed by his clothes.

'Come on you fecking bastards,' he muttered. Burnip cursed in the same tongue his father had used with him and his older brothers as they had toiled on what passed for farmland in Kilkenny. The mists and fog had helped to pile misery upon misery on that godforsaken land and being reminded of it didn't lift his mood.

His only companions for the last few hours had been deer and hares, curious as to why he was sat atop his horse while hidden amongst loosely spaced trees at the side of the road.

In front of him, on the saddle and nestled between his legs, was an oil lantern. It was lit, its flame turned low so as not to burn too hot. He used it to keep his hands warm, as cold, stiffened fingers could lead to awkward mishaps such as dropped pistols. Occasionally he lifted the lantern and held it towards sounds coming from the heath, but it was only nervous hares or a badger wandering by with food on its mind.

He checked his two ageing flintlocks for what seemed like the hundredth time, making sure his powder hadn't also succumbed to the pervasive damp of the mist. He was no stranger to firing his guns and so knew to keep them in good order at all times. Damp powder was only one in a lengthy list of problems that a flintlock could present, and which could result in a highwayman with his head blown off by a coachman's shotgun or his chest run through with a sabre by some indignant gentleman, or the final indignity, a five minute swing in the wind at Tyburn.

Burnip had quickly come to the realisation that victims who were left dead were far less likely to identify a man like him, than if allowed to go on their way once his business was concluded and as an individual who was short, swarthy and whose pock marked face carried physical reminders of a terrible bout of smallpox in his youth, he was in no pleasant way instantly memorable.

His preference for a more dreadful end to his work set him aside from most other highwaymen, who would shoot only as a last resort and usually when in need of escape. Or so the pamphlets and newspapers would have you believe, telling nonsense stories of dashing Robin Hoods and gentlemen thieves who only inconvenienced the aristocracy. Burnip couldn't help but spit on the ground at this.

Because of proclivity for murder he couldn't engage with others of his trade, he was excluded from their high-minded little circle of gossip. They considered themselves to be above the likes of mere footpads and cutthroats and kept their distance as though even acknowledging such as he might taint their heroic persona.

The likes of Turpin and Swift he knew for a fact had some sort of communication going on. They would make sure they didn't cross into each other's routes and offer advice on which roads were seeing the Kingsmen patrolling them and which might see a good bit of high value traffic.

He hated those fops. How many were there now? How many bloody *'legends of the road.'* Swift, la Roche, Moonlight Bill, Danny Boy, the 'Fox O' North' and of course the thug Turpin, who had been placed on a pedestal as if some chivalric hero of Arthurian legend.

'Damned bleedin' dandies,' he cursed.

'They ain't no better n' me. Just cos they put on airs and graces, just cos they might actually let their quarry loose from the trap.'

'Ponces,' Burnip growled as his thoughts simmered to the surface.

He looked up, and saw stars through a new gap in the mist. He considered giving it up for the night, but three hours was a long time to have gotten cold and miserable and to have nothing to show for it.

This was part of the drawback of working The Devil's Road, wondering if anyone would be brave enough to cross it. It had a reputation. But unlike the Great North Road which was widely known by travellers for its footpads, highwayman and road gangs, this route, which took its traffic to the west of London and on to Bristol or Devon, was feared more for its disappearances. Tales abounded of travellers setting out never to be heard of again, of carriages and carts arriving at villages and towns without driver or passengers.

Burnip knew the superstitions had grown from the times of plague and civil war and every other calamity that had fallen upon simple people of the last few hundred years. It was not inaccurate to state that some of the smaller villages still clung to their pagan roots, some to religions far older. But the truth, beyond pure wild exaggeration, was that the land all about this road - which was more of a dirt track - was beset with peat bogs, swamps and muddy streams that could turn to rivers in the blink of an eye. A traveller, even a driver could get lost just turning around if he took a pause for a piss in the fog.

Burnip preferred to work this stretch so he didn't have contend with the patrols of Kingsmen. These bands of soldiers were now almost a fixture out of London on the North Road. He also wanted to avoid the other highwaymen and footpads too. He had seen off more than one indignant oaf claiming to have priority over some stretch or other that he had also chosen to hunt in search of a prize.

He had put a knife to one of them only recently. *Red Rich*, he had called himself. Only the real dandies named themselves, they were the worst kind of Frenchified mollies.

'*Rich had been Red alright,*' the thought cheered him a little and he chuckled. '*Once I'd cut his throat from ear to Frenchified ear.*'

A sound in the distance caused him to cut short his reminiscence. The unmistakable clattering of wooden wheels upon the rough but compressed dirt road.

'Business at last!' Burnip grumbled to a hare sat beside a clump of brambles.

He turned up the flame of his lantern but hid the light within his soggy cloak. He usually relied on moonlight to ensure that he could both see his target and for the target to see him but tonight it would have to be the lantern thanks to the mist bank. 'Moonlight

Bill' earned his name for only performing when a full moon was clear in the sky. Burnip couldn't afford to be so picky.

It was hard to rob a coach that just went hurtling straight past you and very dangerous in the dark. Better to let your pistols and your intent be seen by the driver. Also easier to shoot them once they had come to a halt. The lantern would have to suffice.

As the rumble of wheels grew louder Burnip kicked his heels into the flanks of his horse. Not strictly *his* horse though as he had stolen the beast in town earlier. It wasn't a good animal by any means, definitely not one he would get good coin for later on. It was a thin and mangy thing but had been conveniently left where he could take it without being noticed.

Reluctantly the horse stepped forward. Burnip positioned himself in the centre of the road and waited.

While working at this hour of the morning had its drawbacks, to start with it was bloody cold, it was very dark and there were far too few travellers to assault, there were advantages too. The vehicles that came his way tended to move at a slower pace, poor visibility - especially in mist - contributing to a cautious speed.

A coachman would rarely risk his life for his fare but if he had a bit of time to line up a shot he would certainly deliver a blast from the obligatory shotgun sat by his side. In the dark this was never going to happen, allowing Burnip to feel confident in getting close up and with his pistols primed.

As the coach neared he turned up the oil lantern so its glow was as bright as its wick would allow, the heat of it upon his cool, damp face was welcome. Burnip didn't wear a mask. Many of the dandies did but as he wouldn't leave anyone alive to describe him he didn't feel it was required. Besides he had no doubt that his awful, cratered visage with its gravestone teeth and narrow, yellowed eyes added to his fearsome presentation.

He hoisted the lantern high and pointed a pistol towards the sound of the approaching carriage. He couldn't see it yet but had no doubt that it would be within sight his light. The driver would have two choices, attempt to drive on or stop. To continue meant to risk there being an obstacle in the road that would destroy the legs of his horses and possibly injure both himself and his passengers.

Burnip kicked at the nag's flank and yanked upon its bridle, the horse lifted to its back legs and whinnied. He was impressed that the ragged animal managed to perform the theatrics.

The coaches' lights, one either side, clearly bigger than the small one that Burnip carried, shone brightly in the mist as the carriage finally drew near enough. Burnip was pleased to hear the almost immediate slowing of the wheels. Sometimes a driver, especially at this time of the morning would be sleepy and stopping in time became a close call.

He placed his lantern on a hook he had made especially for the purpose. It held the lamp away from the horse and gave him light by which to work.

With the coach slowing Burnip was able to begin his assault. If the driver tried to speed up again, realising it was a hold-up, it would be too late. Even the tired old bag of bones he rode would be enough for him to keep pace and fire at the driver or the passenger's carriage, whichever Burnip felt appropriate.

'Stand and Deliver!' he shouted in his most commanding voice, 'or ye'll be ridin' with the Devil this night!'

The vehicle came to a complete stop before he had taken position. Burnip kept one pistol trained on the faint outline of the driver and one towards the door of the carriage. He used his feet, booted and sporting iron spurs, to guide the subservient horse. In truth he had few talents or abilities but he could work a horse well, was a good shot and had a steady hand.

Closer, the mist allowed him to see more of the coachman. He seemed tall, even seated, his jacket was thick and looked quite fine. This was good. If the staff were dressed well then the occupants would likely be very wealthy. He wore a dark, possibly black neckerchief about his mouth and nose, required in the cold, damp weather to avoid all manner of illness. On his head the coachman wore a fine tricorn hat. Burnip wondered if it might have fancy braiding as he had been considering obtaining one for himself.

The coachman didn't reach for a weapon or drop the reins of the two fine beasts that worked his vehicle. He only turned his head slowly as he followed Burnip crossing to the side of him.

'Drop the reins fella,' Burnip shouted. The coachman didn't comply. Instead he remained still, only watching from within the shadow of his hat.

'Drop 'em I say or I'll make a hole in that fancy coat.'

The coachman said and did nothing.

Burnip looked towards the carriage door. There was no sound or movement. He wasn't in the mood for pissing about with some dumbstruck coachman. He had hoped he'd be able to keep the driver's jacket free of damage but would have to make do with his hat. He fired a single round into the man's heart.

The driver shuddered a little. His head dipped, his body followed, collapsing to the side as though he had fallen to sleep. The horses shuffled a little but didn't start at the noise.

Burnip moved his horse towards the door of the coach. He put the spent pistol into a holster at his hip and pulled a second from the leather brace across his chest.

'Open the door in there.' Burnip shouted again. 'Your man at the horses wanted to be a hero, don't you go the same way as he.'

The door slowly swung open.

Burnip narrowed his eyes to see who was inside. The light from the lantern fixed to the nag was all that illuminated the interior. He could see a dress, a large and exquisite garment of silk, patterned he thought, with small beads and delicate embroidery. It was a very pale blue, run through with a lighter coloured silk, possibly white. He could see only up to a voluptuous bosom as shadow obscured all from there on. The dress was slim at the waist and the lady who occupied it was clearly blessed above.

Something stirred in Burnip, a warmth in his groin. It had been a while since he had known a woman. The last had been Polly Dwim at the back of Lancaster Street. A passionless rutting with that toothless bitch had given him an itch, he was sure of it. He had paid two coppers for the privilege too. He had meant to follow that up at some point and retrieve his ill spent coin but Polly had a rare large man that looked after her business interests and Burnip didn't fancy tangling with him so let it slide, at least for now.

'Show yerself lady,' Called out, 'no harm need come yer way if yer do as you're told.'

Burnip was already working that bosom out of its confines in his mind. Great smooth things, not the sagging sow teats of Polly Dwim. He licked his lips as the passenger leaned forward into the weak light. He hoped she would be pretty, a princess, but it didn't really matter.

His jaw dropped as the vision looked at him from the gloomy interior. Golden hair, a luxurious pile of locks held in place with a diamond crusted tiara, either side of her face two thick twists curled down to her neck. Her eyes were sultry, flattened a little at the sides like the oriental girls he had seen at the docks, her nose slim, a support for perfectly balanced cheekbones and her lips were full and red with lipstick. Her make-up was powder-white with only a dab of rouge and trace of eyeliner.

She was the most beautiful woman that 'Black' Paul Burnip had ever seen.

For a moment he was without words. They had dried in his throat and stuck to his tongue. He slipped one of his pistols back into its brace satisfied that there was no one else in the carriage. This would be a special night. He would move the vehicle off the road and drive it a little into the heath. He would have this woman for the rest of the morning. This sort of thing didn't happen very often and he intended to make the most of it.

His mind spun with a score of fantasies he would realise with this goddess. He barely considered what valuables she might be carrying because she was prize enough for the moment.

He licked at his lips again and the sensation of his tongue rolling over rough stubble prodded him to action. He waved the pistol.

'Sit yourself down my dear, I'm goin to lead the carriage off the road so as we don't have someone runnin into the back o' yer.' Burnip couldn't help but grin a little, pleased at his little ruse to keep her calm.

Yet, of all the expressions he had expected the look of calm, almost pleasant interest in what was going on was not one of them. The beautiful, golden haired woman did not immediately sit back, instead her eyes looked Paul over, from his boots to his filthy, worn hat.

'If ye'll sit ma'am,' he repeated but a little more forcefully.

He was very willing to make her sit, if that's what was required, although he would be careful not to hurt her face as he wanted to look at it while he took her, at least for a bit.

He was about to add that 'it would all be over shortly' when the nightmare began. The change was so fast that Burnip saw no transition from the lightly powdered face of an angel to the gaping maw, filled with ragged teeth that became her entire face. It was open wide, impossibly wide, almost a circle of raw pulsing red, encircled with those awful little teeth.

He didn't have time to produce a scream and couldn't if he had, his breath was caught in his chest. Something twitched in the centre of the hideous, gaping mouth. Burnip felt a sudden intense pain in his head and his vision blurred as tears sprang from his eyes. Tears and blood he found, as he reached up with his free hand to clear them. He then discovered that he was one eye less than he had a moment ago.

Now the scream came. The pain pushed his trapped breath out of the way and Burnip bawled at the top of his lungs. He looked at his hand with his remaining eye as he pulled it away from his face, it was slick with his blood and his cheeks warmed as it flowed over them.

He looked back to the thing in the carriage, it was still leaning forward, as though to get a better view, the dress, the hefty bosom all the same, but the maw seemed to shudder and flap inside while it remained stretched out into the horrible, vicious circle of teeth. He knew that it was consuming his eye. Something had lashed out of that hellish opening and plucked it out of his head.

Some of his senses came back to him and he pointed his pistol directly at the nightmare but before he could pull the trigger something gripped his wrist and tugged it away. Instinctively his finger pulled at the trigger and the pistol discharged uselessly into the road.

Burnip looked in shock at the hand gripping his wrist, following the fine thick cloth of sleeve until he came face to face with the coachman he had dispatched only minutes ago. Dark inhuman eyes stared at him with indifference. He could see the hole torn into the man's jacket, perfectly placed over where his heart would be.

'No, no, no,' Black Paul yelled. He tried to pull his wrist away but the coachman's grip was vice-like. Instinct managed to surface through the flood of fear and panic that was engulfing him, he reached for a knife he kept in his belt and in a swift, dextrous manoeuvre lifted it enough to deliver a solid blow when he brought it down onto the arm of the driver. It passed through the jacket sleeve and rammed solidly into flesh. Burnip felt the blade graze bone.

But the driver didn't flinch. Instead his grip tightened so much that Paul felt his wrist might actually snap. The dark eyes didn't move from Pauls as he felt his bones mash together. Not losing his innate sense of survival he lifted the knife and began to stab rapidly at the arm. Blood began to pour from the sleeve but the driver kept his excruciating hold upon him.

Suddenly it went dark and a familiar pain tore through Burnip's skull once again. His remaining eye was gone. He held his fisted hand, that was still gripping the knife, to where his eye should be. Blood flowed from this new, debilitating wound.

His mount, the tired old thing, didn't move, it only waited patiently as though it knew there was no danger to it from these things. It would let them be about their business and then amble back to the city.

Burnip couldn't see the thing in the carriage but felt it moving towards him. A cool hand slid delicate fingers around his jaw. He sensed a tightening of them as they gripped at his chin and teeth. In one swift movement his jaw was torn from his face.

He couldn't produce words or even a scream, instead he gagged as he tried to plead to 'the blessed Lord God who watches and protects.'

He hadn't said prayers in a long, long time. As a child he had done them, as he sat, hunched under the stairs after a usual beating from his father. He begged God to help him, to strike his father down. In the end he had done it himself. It had seemed far more expedient than waiting for help from above.

As the shock and numbness, which he might have been grateful for later, faded he felt himself being pulled from the nag and landed with barely noticeable impact onto the muddy road. He still had strength and flailed about him with the knife as the cast iron grip on his wrist was gone.

Burnip sensed that the creature in the beautiful dress and the masked driver stood about him even without his eyes to see and knew that his pathetic attempts to defend himself were being mocked by the things that stood about him.

Suddenly strong hands gripped his ankles and he was being dragged, away from the road. He knew was being moved onto the heath, out of sight of anyone who was brave or foolish enough to travel The Devil's Road at this ungodly hour.

As his body was pulled through the damp grass and over the uneven turf, far enough into the heath that the mist would mask them from the road Burnip knew that it was there they would have their way with him for the rest of the morning.

FORT HOPE

First impressions meant a lot to Quint Zachary, he had relied heavily on them as a cop and perhaps to a greater extent now as a survivor. That his first impression of the man opposite him was that he was a snake made him uneasy.

The man had the usual look of a person who had walked through hell. Eyes wide, constantly alert, weather beaten skin and a helter-skelter diet. There was nothing strange about that, in fact had those signs been missing Quint would have been even more suspicious of him. But there was something.

They sat across from each other with a modest table between them. It was a simple piece of furniture that Quint had found in a store during a foraging mission. The store had been difficult to gain access to as it had been heavily fortified, so much so that Quint had thought it might still be occupied but he had been wrong on this, it was empty of anyone alive, but once inside it was obvious that many groups had used the place for temporary refuge at least.

The table had caught his attention when he saw that names had been carved into it, many alongside dates and here and there messages had been written with a marker pen. One in particular had caught his eye, '*Even at the end there is hope, for an end signifies a new beginning,*' and it was then he knew that he had to bring the table into what at the time was known as 'the camp.' Now it was Fort Hope.

As the man, who said his name was Preston, sipped at the tall glass of water which had been provided for him Quint slowly ran his finger through a capital letter R that had been deeply cut into the surface of his table directly in front of where he rested his hands. He didn't take his eyes off his guest.

'Thank you,' Preston said as he finished the last of the water. 'I needed that, it's been a while since I could risk drinking a whole glass.'

'No problem,' Quint replied.

All guests were offered water. It was a courtesy that had grown into something of the tradition over the last eight years.

Anyone who came to the door of his community and offered no violence at being refused entry would receive a meal if supplies allowed and a glass of water to help them on their way. They were after all never short of water.

'Baxter said you wanted to speak to me. Said you had something that I would be interested in, seemed excited too. You must have a hell of a pitch mister because talking your way past Baxter is something of an art form.'

Preston smiled good naturedly. 'Well sir, it's not every day that you will hear a story like mine.'

'Ohh, I don't know. I've heard a lot of stories.'

'Like I said, not like mine,' Preston said confidently.

Preston was clean shaven which Quint found at odds with how a man should look these days. A man shouldn't have time to shave regularly. He trimmed his beard every week, there was no need to abandon all outward signs of civility, he wasn't a savage, but as almost all of the trappings of a 21st century lifestyle had fallen by the wayside he could see no reason to sharpen a blade only to bare his cheeks.

But it told him things at least. It told him that Preston was a man who wanted to make an impression, and that he must have a blade of some kind that he kept razor sharp. This was fine. No harm in looking good when trying to gain the good favour of a camp or enclave, and knives were practically mandatory. Even little Jessica, Doc Bray's daughter, twelve years old, had a knife.

'All right, but first I need to ask you a few things, get to know a little about you. You alright with that?'

'Of course.' Preston replied easily. He spoke and he sat like a man who hadn't a care in the world, another thing that made Quint's shoulders bunch. *'Talking to this man is like having ants crawling over me,'* he thought.

'Fire away.' Preston said and placed his hands palm down on the table.

'Ok. Where you from, originally?'

'Florida. Tallahassee,' Preston replied.

'Florida? I won't say that I we haven't had people from further afield but that's still a long way to travel and reach us.'

'Yes sir,' Preston nodded in agreement, 'you see, when it happened the first thing I did was head west. I'd hoped it would be clear, y'know, that it would be different.

'Yeah, I get ya.' Quint said.

Doc Bray, father of the camps youngest resident and wielder of knives had done the exact same thing, but from Canada.

'I travelled to a few of the cities on the way but it soon became apparent that they were all no go areas, I mean, they were *infested* man, so after that I stuck to back roads, towns, y'know, where there would be fewer people.'

Quint continued to offer light nods of agreement. He hadn't travelled as far, but the basic scenario was the same. He had seen Chicago burning to ground and he had experienced horrors in Detroit that he hoped to God he would never live through again.

'What did you do? I mean before.'

'I was a chemist,' Preston said plainly.

Quint raised his eyebrows, he hated to show his hand this early but a chemist was of great interest to him.

'You don't say?' he said, and stopped rubbing his finger into the tables chiselled gouges.

'Yes sir, you have to understand that in professional terms I was still only a journeyman. I was twenty-six when it all went down and had only just finished university.'

Quint gave himself a mental pat on the back for having gauged the man's age to the very year, if what he was saying was truthful, and at the moment he had no reason to think he wasn't then he was thirty-four years old.

'I had just started work at a pharmacy, in a junior capacity of course, then… well, my career prospects changed as I'm sure you can imagine.'

Quint could imagine. What a year that had been. He had been liasing with the D.E.A as senior detective, he was probably two or three months away from a promotion and had already begun looking for a new apartment.

It had all gone south for him during a raid on a meth lab which his team had managed to pinpoint. Flanked by D.E.A agents and wearing enough body armour to give Robocop a run for his money they had stormed the derelict meat-processing plant only to find everyone dead. From the looks of it one of the Einsteins in the gang had got his ingredients wrong and gassed the place.

Bodies lay about the room and although there was an extractor fan, still running, it was clear even to Quint that it wouldn't have been powerful enough to pull out a sudden cloud of toxic vapour. It had been amateur hour in there. No gas masks, no safety gloves. How these guys had progressed past cutting rat poison into heroin was beyond him. Still they were the coroner's problem now.

While the D.E.A agents secured the scene he and his partner Russo strolled outside to consider what to do with the free time they would have in the afternoon thanks to the ineptitude of their suspects. That was when the screams had begun.

'But you know the basics? You could operate in a pharmacy?' Quint said, his interest in Preston had taken a leap from wary to verging on excited.

Basics? Well…yes of course, I mean I may have sold myself a little short there sir…'

'It's Quint, Quint Zachary, but I do appreciate the sentiment.'

Preston smiled and allowed a little relief to show on his face.

'Well, ah, Quint. While I stated that I was a journeyman I was of course already a fully qualified chemist, my training was to be how to implement my skills in a practical manner. In this instance in an actual pharmacy.'

'Well I'll tell you Preston this community has a fine practioner in Doctor Bray, and we have a bunch of nurses who have seen to it that we haven't lost a soul to anything other than natural causes in two years,' Quint leaned back into his chair a little.

'But I'll be straight up with you son, we could use a chemist. We have good relations with a number of other communities and our bargaining power with them would be increased considerably if we could offer medicines to them.'

'And that sir…' Preston raised a finger, then added 'I'm sorry, Quint, that is why I have come to you and this community with an even greater gift.'

Quint blinked and sobered a little. He was always on the lookout for people who could further the community, people with skills, artisans, craftsman, scientists and especially those who worked in the field of medicine. The whole point of these face to face meetings was to discover if any of the countless survivors who came knocking on their door had anything about he could use. It was infrequent that this was the case.

It was as though the only people who were smart or charmed enough to survive were salesmen or data analysts or marketing executives. A sanitation operative would be more useful to Fort Hope than any of those guys, but every now and then a carpenter or a plumber or a mechanic would appear.

Yet even these were not guaranteed a home and a place in Fort Hope. This was where his own skill set came in. He could spot an alcoholic, a junkie and a racist with just a polite conversation. While their talents might be useful, and he would hire them under supervision, they could not be offered a home.

He had been close to not liking Preston. He had no reason, the man didn't strike him as a drunk or any kind of user but his gut instinct had said 'No' and it usually served him well.

'He's a chemist!'

Quint's reasoning bore down on his vague emotional rejection and highlighted what a person with his talents could do to further push their world closer to what had once been normality.

'A greater gift?' Quint echoed.

'Far greater,' Preston's whole demeanour changed. His shoulders straightened and he clasped his hands together on the table. 'Let me ask you something, if you don't mind Quint?'

'Fire away,' Quint replied mimicking Preston, but careful not to appearing mocking.

'What is the biggest threat we face other than those things out there?'

Quint thought for a moment. 'Disease I guess, I mean starvation should things go bad, but it all comes down to that same thing in the end.'

'Really? You think that?' Preston said quizzically.

'Yeah, I think so,' Quint replied.

'I don't. I think that the biggest, most active threat we have is ourselves, other people.'

Quint was interested in this. It was something that he had discussed many times with Baxter.

'Go on,' he said.

'You must be wondering why I've been travelling across the land, why I haven't found some camp or group to take me in, I mean with what I can offer right?'

'It had crossed my mind,' Quint said, although oddly, it hadn't.

'Because of trust Quint. Because I've seen how other places are run, some are nothing more than despotisms, others chaotic free for all's. I've seen whites only, blacks only, Hispanic only settlements,' Preston raised his hands as if in surrender, 'Did you know there's a Scientologist town just fifty miles from here?'

'Uh huh. I know about that camp, folks around here called it Space Mountain. Got overrun last I heard.'

'Oh yeah?' Preston said and made no attempt to disguise his lack of care about that, 'The thing is Quint I heard about this place, about your town, about *FORT HOPE.*'

He lay his hands back down onto the table. 'And I knew that this is where it would start.'

'Where what would start?'

'The rebuilding of civilisation,' Preston said.

Quint smiled and uttered an apologetic, 'heh.'

'Son I... *Preston*, we can *use* your talent, believe me we really can, and I'm sure you know that, but... what I have in mind is something a little more modest. Better meds for our people, supplies that we can trade with Camp Hooley in the northeast and Rivertown in the south. I'm afraid the rebuilding of civilisation is going to have to wait a while.'

Preston said nothing but looked at Quint with searching eyes.

'I'm sorry, but that's the way it is.' Quint said.

Preston shuffled his chair a little closer to the table and leaned in as though he had a secret to share.

'Quint are you a man of your word?'

Surprised at this Quint thought for a moment before giving his answer. He was not above lying, in the right circumstances, and if he thought it was for the right reasons, but it wasn't something he took lightly. He could be hard, ruthless even, he would admit to that, but it was something he had learned to be for the sake of the community. For all that though, despite the occasional lie and a pragmatic approach to his new existence he believed he was a good man.

'I believe I am. I think that a man who can't hold true to his own word isn't really man at all. He's just vapours that drift with whatever breeze blows against him.'

Preston nodded, 'Good, that's what I had heard, and so with that in mind I want you to give me your word that you will remain calm and open minded about what I am about to tell you.'

Quint narrowed his eyes and again the feeling that there was something not quite right about Preston stole over him. He came over as normal enough, if a little confident, he didn't have a beard to disguise his expression and all he had seen was... just another survivor. Naturally he was unarmed too. Baxter would have stripped him of weapons, besides which he *was* carrying his pistol and had a Bowie knife in his boot. Couple this with the fact that he was almost half the man's width again with muscle and maintained a vigorous martial training program, being attacked was the least of his worries.

'Are you going to give me reason to get mad at you Preston?' Quint asked carefully.

'Not mad no, but you may get excited,' Preston replied.

Quint hated people playing with words and he felt that this was what Preston was doing.

'Alright,' Quint said.

'I have your word?'

'You have my word. What have you got to say?'

Preston took a breath and rolled up the sleeve of his jacket. 'You ever have anyone survive a bite?' he asked as he pushed the sleeve past his elbow.

'No,' Quint said plainly.

'What's the longest you've ever seen anyone last that's been bitten.'

Quint looked to the side as he thought about it and then turned back to Preston.

'Depends. On the severity I suppose. I saw a guy get bit on the ear one time, didn't even take it off, just cut it a little. We thought he had gotten lucky, but he was dead within eight hours. Turned about an hour later.'

'Eight hours,' Preston repeated.

'Give or take fifteen minutes,' Quint said. 'Of course if they die from a more severe wound that's a different matter it can be minutes at best.'

Preston nodded again. Then lay his bare arm down onto the table so that Quint could see it clearly.

'I got bit,' Preston said.

The marks were plain to see. A ring of crooked indentations that had scarred the flesh. There were a couple of places that were paler than others, where small chunks of skin had come away.

Quint's reaction was instinctive. As soon as he realised what had been said and what he was looking at he pushed himself away from the table, almost falling over the chair as it crashed behind him.

'Jesus Christ!' he shouted and whipped his pistol out from its holster levelling it directly at Preston's face.

Preston remained sat, his arm still lying upon the table.

'You gave me your word Quint,' he said with a hint of annoyance.

'What the hell do you think you are doing coming in here bit?' Quint shouted.

'Six weeks ago,' Preston said.

What?

'I was bitten six weeks ago,' Preston said.

'Impossible.' Quint closed on Preston a little, moving around the fallen chair. He kept his pistol squarely on its target.

'Look at the wound Quint, its healed or at least healing. Damn thing caught me out as I was looking through a department store.'

Quint looked a little more carefully. There were no actual cuts and almost no redness. Any other bite he had seen rapidly became a mess of raw, angry tissue.

'Six weeks?' he asked again.

'That's not all,' Preston said, 'any chance you could put that thing down, to your side at least?'

Quint hesitated but then lowered the pistol. He considered calling for others, this room, the interview room was part of three other connected offices. He used it to keep visitors separate from the main section of the Fort, until he was happy that they should enter. The other offices had people in them who could come if he called. They might even come anyway, if they heard him shout.

'Right, now listen I'm going to remove my jacket and then take off my T-shirt, OK?' Preston said, careful not to move his hands or shoulders.

Quint remained still for a moment. Then nodded.

Slowly Preston pushed his chair back from the table and rose to standing. With exquisite calm he pulled his arms out of his jacket and then placed it onto the table. This done he turned his back to Quint.

'I'm going to take off my T-shirt. Don't you fire that thing at me, you gave me your word.'

He couldn't see Quint nod but began to lift his t-shirt off.

Quint immediately saw the ring of tooth marks around his right shoulder. These must have been deeper, a more savage bite, but they too were old, very old, as the skin had completely scarred now.

'You see it?' Preston asked.

Quint offered Preston another unseen nod and then said 'Yes,' in a quiet voice.

Preston turned and began to put the t-shirt back on.

'I got bit eight years ago, I guess I was one of the first. I was rushed to hospital, it was one of my colleagues who attacked me and he was shot by the cops. Apparently I died on the way to the hospital but the paramedics jump-started me back to life, and I mean to *real* life. I was in there overnight but was discharged the next day, of course come that evening all hell had broken loose. It got bad fast in Florida.'

'Are you sure the guy was…'

'He was as dead as Dillinger Quint, he was covered head to foot in blood and someone had stuck a scalpel in his eye. It was still in there when they shot him apparently.'

'The defibrillator?'

'I don't know,' Preston shrugged into his jacket. 'There are a lot of variables, I've gone over them in my mind time and time again but without some serious research I can't say for sure.'

'You lived though,' Quint said, almost as though he were far away in his thoughts.

'I lived. And that's not all.'

Quint shook his head as though he had not heard correctly.

'That's not all?'

'They don't see me,' Preston said.

'Don't… how do you mean.'

'They either don't see me or don't care that I'm around because they don't attack me.'

Quint paused, 'Your arm?'

'That was a frenzy. Like I said, I was caught in a department store, only the thing is I wasn't alone. Some group was in there too, just nomads I think. Anyway those bastards came streaming in after these guys and it just went crazy, they frenzied…you've seen that before right?

Quint nodded, he had seen it. Sometimes they went utterly ballistic, as though the blood fuelled some sort of rage inside them, rather than just attacking to eat they would rip and tear at anything they could, even each other.

'One of them just clamped down on me as I was trying to get through the mayhem. Fortunately, I had my knife ready and I was able to finish it. Hurt like the Christ though.'

'You just walked away?'

'Yup,' Preston said. 'Truth? I spent five years just like everyone else, running, hiding, terrified. Only in the last couple of years did I realise that the only thing I had to worry about was other people.'

Quint caught a laugh in his mouth. The absurdity of it.

'They can't see you.'

'No sir.'

Now Quint laughed. He holstered his pistol, 'I'll be damned.'

Preston smiled. 'It's something. It sure is.'

'Son…' Quint shook his head, 'Son if what you are saying is true, and I pray to whatever God's there are out there watching all of this that it is, then we can… we can *move on*. We can build a city, not just a town, we can get whatever we need. My God if we can figure out what makes you tick!'

'That's why I'm here Quint,' Preston said.

Quint lifted the fallen chair from the floor and pushed it under the table.

'We need to… I need to see this. You understand that right?' Quint said, serious now but unable to hide the excitement in his voice.

'I understand completely and I'm ready to prove whatever you need to satisfy you. I'll dance a jig in the middle of a graveyard if that's what it takes.'

'My God,' Quint said, shaking his head and flexing his hands.

'Listen, could I get another drink of water because believe it or not you are quite a scary guy even without a gun in your hand,' Preston said, but smiled as he did so.

'What... oh sure, look I'm sorry but I gotta...'

'Hey, no of course, this is serious and I knew that it was going to freak you out. Trust me I didn't know what the hell was going on when I realised myself. Look, get two glasses man, let's... let's drink to this. I mean, I hope that this will be *something*, y'know?'

'Yeah of course. Listen. Do you drink for real? Because I have a bottle of Bourbon in my office and I sure could do with a shot.'

'I think it would be rude to refuse,' Preston said cheerfully.

'I'll be right back,' Quint turned and left the room.

Preston heard him walk quickly to one of the other offices. He sat back into his chair and reached down, sliding out a section of the heel of his shoe. It was a simple deception, merely a tray of sorts cut into the thick rubber and easily disguised by the mud and dust that covered them. From it he took a small bag and a slip of paper.

Quickly but carefully he allowed a small amount of powder to spill from the bag and on the square of paper. After returning the bag to its tiny drawer with a practiced hand he folded the paper over the powder and clipped it between his fingers. A small amount of the dust escaped but Preston was happy that there was sufficient for the task at hand.

He stood as Quint returned carrying two shot glasses in one hand and a bottle in the other. He placed the glasses down and raised the bottle so that Preston could see the label.

'E.H Taylor,' Quint said with a smile, 'I've been saving this for a special occasion and I hope I'm right in believing that this is it.'

Preston picked up the glasses. 'Will you do you the honors Mr Zachary?'

'I surely will,' Quint replied, and poured an equal measure into both.

He placed the bottle down onto the table and held his glass towards Preston.

'To hope and the future,' Quint said.

'I'll drink to that,' Preston replied and knocked back the bourbon in time with Quint.

'Sit, please,' Preston said. 'I'll tell you about what I think we can do now.'

Quint dragged out the chair and sat. His head was reeling with thoughts. The first thing was of course to make sure that Preston wasn't just some whack job. He believed him, he believed his story about the bites about being invisible to *them*, the man had spoken clearly and with conviction, his eyes had not wandered as they would if he was making up some romance.

Still, he had to be sure. He and Baxter would take Preston out with them and see if what he claimed was a fact.

'But God, if it's true…'

Quint's thoughts froze at the same time as his fingers.

He felt as though he had been pushed in the back, and then his muscles locked. He tried to move his jaw but couldn't and his tongue felt like a thick, moist sock in his mouth.

'You alright Quint? You've gone a little red,' Preston said, dropping his head a little so that he could look into Quint's eyes.

Quint couldn't reply, he couldn't move at all. His fingers still gripped the small empty glass.

'It's alright,' Preston said calmly, 'you've been drugged. It's good for about ten minutes, maybe a little less for a fellow your size. After the muscle seizure wears off you would just feel a little sore, but that won't be an issue today.'

Preston stood and moved to the door. He looked out and could neither see nor hear anyone. He returned to Quint and stood at his side. He reached to Quint's holster and took his pistol, then knelt to get at the Bowie knife.

'Nice. You keep this sharp,' he said as he admired the blade.

'Now, I'm going to fill you in on all the bits that I missed out during our little interview. I'm going to do this Quint because I want you to understand just how pointless all of this has been.' Preston waved the blade of the Bowie knife around to indicate the camp.

'You see, unlike you I like all this. I've liked it since pretty much day one. Not when I thought I was going to be eaten alive of course, but y'know, once I figured out that I was… special.'

He stood and moved around the table slowly. Quint couldn't move his eyes to follow. Instead they began to water as he also couldn't blink.

'I can have, and do, anything I like. The only danger to me is people like you. People who want to make me fix what they see as their broken world. It's pretty much the same everywhere I've been. There's some guy, it's always some guy, who thinks I'm going to make him the King of America or something, but then he drops his guard and I make him my bitch.'

He stopped and turned to Quint.

'You're my bitch today Mr Zachary,' Preston could see that drool was pouring from Quint's mouth, he had fallen forward a little due to the weight of his upper body.

'Today you and I are going to go through this place like the proverbial plague. You see, you are now patient zero, and from you I will create my own little army, made entirely of your own people. I'll take what and who I like, and then I'll move on as I've done many times before. I'll prevent people like you from bringing back the civilisation that tried to stop me existing Quint. You have to understand and accept that this is a world for monsters now.'

Preston moved behind Quint and reached under his chin with the Bowie knife.

'I'm very pleased that you had this, but then, everyone carries a knife these days don't they?'

With a slow but strong action Preston pulled the blade of the knife around Quint's throat. A gout of thick, dark blood immediately began to pump out of the wound.

Quint couldn't see the cut, and the blade was so sharp he could barely feel his skin paring open, there was a slight pressure as Preston cut through his windpipe. He could see his blood as it was splashing onto the table in front him, filling the chiselled words and names.

Preston was talking but he couldn't hear what he was saying, there was a loud rushing sensation in his ears. His body began to spasm as his system reacted to being choked and drained at the same time. He could see where he had carved his own name. Just underneath the message of hope that had inspired him to bring together the people of this community.

Preston held him by the hair to keep him steady as he died. It didn't take long and when it was done he returned to his chair and waited for Quint to turn.

BARRY'S BOOKS

Part One

The books had been hidden. Barry was certain of that. If he hadn't been required to take a pickaxe to the floor of the old man's basement, he would never have found them. People who want to show off their book collection usually don't cover it with concrete.

There had been a leak in one of the properties that he was looking after and that was how it had started. His flashlight had revealed the problem as he swept its beam down the stairs to the basement and into the gloom. There, a pool of water had been illuminated in its ghostly light. Barry reckoned it was only a couple of inches deep which was a minor blessing and it lay silent and still which was also positive.

There appeared to be nothing else down there. Not a stick of furniture or even an old lampshade but, shallow and free of debris or not as far as Barry was concerned it was just a rectangular expanse of total ball ache.

He had called his boss Mr Singh to ask him what to do. 'Find the bloody leak' Singh had barked in his thick Pakistani accent. Barry's, 'K boss' was answered with the 'beep beep' of the call ending. 'Wanker' Barry said to no one.

He moved about the house looking for the stop taps and checked that each one was properly turned off, which they all appeared to be. He then went to his van and swapped his steel-toe boots for a pair of knee high Wellingtons. Unsure of exactly what course of action to take down there he grabbed a shovel, his safety helmet with a small but strong light fixed to it, and his pickaxe.

Barry hated Mr Singh. He liked the job well enough but Singh was an arrogant and impatient prick. Always on his case, never a good word to say about anyone or anything. Singh's main business was repossessions but Barry didn't get involved with the repo side of things; they had a whole other team that did that. There were some big lads in that team. Not like him. 'Pipsqueak' his Dad had called him, 'skin n' bones', *softlad.*

The team he was a part of was Property Management and Singh liked to remind them that they were the least profitable part of the company. His job was to check the vacated properties for damage and general wear and tear until they were sold. Keeping the gardens in order, fixing any minor issues like broken windows (usually boarded) and occasionally giving a few rooms a lick of paint. It was basic stuff and that suited him just fine.

Floods were not so basic though. They came in two varieties, burst pipes and 'the bloody weather'. Neither were fun to deal with but of the two but weather floods were the worst. He would often find himself clearing away mud, shit and dead animals. Singh would never call anyone in extra to do this. Mean bastard as he was.

This one looked OK as far as it went. The water was not visibly rising so he reasoned that the leak must be slight. It was perhaps a slim crack or some perforation through the pipe. According to the property report the basement had been fine a week ago when the house had been cleared. This lent weight to the argument for the leak to be minor. He stepped into the water and a muted splash followed.

It took longer than he had anticipated to discover the location of the leak. Each time he moved he had to wait for the water to calm. It was near to the stairs; almost in the corner. He had spotted two trails of bubbles about fifteen inches apart. They were small but constant.

He pondered the situation for a moment. If he dug down and struck a pipe, especially a pipe that was already fractured he could turn the current drama into a crisis. He had nothing on the van to deal with a full on burst. The sensible option would be to call the water authority. They could turn off the street mains and reduce the risk of it getting serious, but this would be costly.

Mr Singh would be all over him if it turned out to be something that could be fixed with sticky tape, of that he was certain. He collected the pickaxe from the bottom of the stairs, marched back to the spot and with grim acceptance began to work at the floor.

Barry knew that something was odd when the concrete had cracked with the first blow from the pick. Under the noise of the splashing water and the thud of the metal tip eating into the surface there had been a 'whumpf' sound.

The helmet light showed that under the still rippling water a very definite outline of a square had become apparent. The blow had caused a single slab of concrete to lift away from the rest of the floor by a couple of millimetres. He squatted down and ran his fingers around the edge of the slab. There was not enough of the piece lifted to gain any kind of grip on it.

He stood, rested the pickaxe against the stairs and brought over the shovel. It was fairly new and its edge was straight and strong. With some considerable effort he managed to wedge the blade down into the middle of one side of the square and then performed a series of pushing wiggling motions. Once the tip was a good inch into the gap he had created he levered the slab upwards. Carefully pushing the handle down and using his foot to hold it in place, Barry gripped the raised edge of the slab and lifted it up. It was not particularly heavy and he managed to flip the piece over with ease.

The helmet light now revealed the top of what appeared to be a box. He assumed it was made of some kind of dark wood, perhaps Mahogany although it was difficult to be sure.

His thoughts raced furiously. A box, buried under the floor in an old fella's house. There could be gems or gold or cash or antiques maybe; *anything* could be in there. He tried to recall what the guy did for a living but then realised that he was *old*, he would have been retired. The house was decent though. Four bedrooms, large living room, double garage. The fitted kitchen was nice. He must have had a few quid to have lived his years out in this place.

A switch clicked in his thoughts. *'Professor.'* His name had been listed as Mr Grace on the inventory forms but there had been mail piled up by the door. *Professor* D. A. Grace. Academic types were always worth a bit.

He squatted again and tried to lift it out of the hole but found it impossible. There was a gap of only about two inches between the earth and the box. He couldn't get a decent grip and succeeded in merely scraping his knuckles.

He went back to the van and looked for something to help extract it from the hole without having to dig more of the floor up.

He had noticed that the box appeared to be tilted a little as if something might be wedged under it or it was on uneven ground. This raised the possibility of getting something under the raised side.

He reached in and pulled out a long length of rope that he used to secure things onto his roof rack. He also grabbed a couple of lengths of wood that could act as props and then hurried back to the basement.

The plan, to loop the rope under the raised side of the box and then to haul it up had been sound in theory, but it had taken him over an hour to finally lift the box high enough. It had also required extremely dextrous footwork to slide a piece of the wood underneath it and keep it there. But lift it he did.

As the box finally lifted free Barry has been at almost ninety degrees to the floor. He could not believe the weight of the thing and every muscle in his body had been stretched to capacity.

The water filled hole suddenly gave up its grip on the box and it fell forward with a dull thud and accompanying splash. The rope now slipped off the bottom and Barry had staggered backwards a little and then fallen flat on his back, his safety had rolled off his head. He shrieked as the cold water rushed into his clothes washed over him.

He quickly got to his feet, shaking his hands and cursing. He snatched the safety hat up from the water and received a further dousing of water as he placed it onto his head. He stood still and silently fumed for a short while.

Now that the box was free of the hole and the water had cooled his excitement a little Barry decided to deal with the leak before he returned to the box. In truth he was a little annoyed with it, as though it had been deliberately obnoxious to him.

As he was already soaked through he decided to just stick his arm into the water filled hole and feel for the pipe. His fingers quickly contacted the solid curve of the pipe. Gently he slid them along the surface and as his did so he could feel the coarseness of disintegrating metal.

Barry could see the old man digging down and hitting the pipe. Realising he could go no further he must have then dropped the box down onto it. With the box being so heavy he might have actually put it in first and then filled it with whatever the contents were. '*Gold, gold, gold.*' No doubt this caused the box the move a little each time and chafe the already weakened metal.

'*Mystery of the slow flood solved,*' Barry thought with some pride.

He withdrew his arm, stood and returned to the van. He changed into the overalls he had in the back for painting work and called the Water Board.

'*Fuck Singh,*' he thought.

He knew that getting the box up the stairs was going to take some effort but he was now ready for it. A determination had steeled his resolve. This box was going to change his life. He knew it.

Part Two

His first thought was that the guy had caught up and smashed him over the head. Barry found himself on his hands and knees, head bowed. This was quickly followed by the sensation of heat on his neck; had he been coshed? It felt like he may have passed out for a moment.

He looked up. About ten feet away was a table, which sported two teacups complete with saucers, two tumbler glasses and a jug of what he assumed to be water. On both sides of the table were two meshed cane chairs, and over all of this a vast umbrella shaded the ground. It looked like a scene from some great house in Colonial India, except…it was all surrounded by desert.

'Desert?'

He snapped his head around, suddenly remembering that he had been running from someone, and was greeted by a blinding Sun that was high and its glare intense. Barry quickly stood. Sand was stuck to his hands and he rubbed them together as he turned 360 degrees to take in his surroundings. This was not a back street of Erdington, Birmingham. *This* was not England.

Other than the table and chairs and of course the umbrella that protected them from the sun there was only sand for miles. Here and there dunes had formed and broke an otherwise flat expanse of brown. It made no sense. He rubbed his hand up and down the back of his head, still suspecting that he had been bashed into unconsciousness. He must be dreaming.

The heat of the sun, the coarseness of the sand, the sheer vividness of his surroundings sat at odds with it being a dream though. Then there was the table and chairs. He made his way over, noting the sand giving way under his footsteps.

As soon as he entered the shade provided by the umbrella sweat burst out of every pore as if it had been in a state of delayed shock. He took off his jacket. If it was a dream then his clothing was the same as he had been wearing when the huge copper had cornered him in the underground car park. As he slipped off the black suit jacket that had already begun to show a layer of dust he checked the label.

James of Saville Row, size 40" Chest. Dry Clean Only.

Yes, that was his. He draped it across the back of the nearest chair and then sat. He noticed that the jug of water had ice cubes in it. There were also two slices of Lime that mingled with them. He took one of the tumblers and filled it from the jug. One of the ice cubes slipped over the edge and landed into the tumbler with a 'splop'.

He took a cautious sip. It was good. Cold and refreshing and the hint of Lime gave it a bittersweet edge. Barry drank the rest in one slug, tipping his head back and allowing the ice cube to drop into his mouth.

As he brought his head back down and crunched on the cube he saw a man approaching his strange oasis. He appeared from the haze so his distance was difficult to judge but it was *not* the copper. This man had neither his build nor his skin colour, but Barry considered bolting from the chair before he got any closer.

'Where to though?'

Barry's eyes darted left and right. Sand, more sand and the boiling hot Sun. He could only think that this place would make for a very dull I Spy game and an even worse hide and seek. The fractured ice cube continued to melt in his mouth. He stayed put.

As the figure approached Barry could see that he wore a suit. It was white or perhaps off-white, the blur produced by the angry heated air made it difficult to tell. His skin was dark but not black, more caramel, and smooth. Barry guessed his age to be around thirty-five to forty, tidily cut black hair was just visible underneath a bright red fez that sported with a golden tassel that hanging lazily over the right side.

The fez alone convinced him that this was in fact a dream. No one wore a fez, not since Tommy Cooper. With no other thoughts on how to deal with the situation Barry sat and crunched on the last pieces of solid ice, grinding his jaw like a cow, waiting for the man to arrive.

The man in the Fez reached the umbrella's rim and ducked under it to enter to shade. He pulled back the other cane chair a little and sat, taking a moment to brush away a little dust from his knee. He smiled. He had been smiling as he approached but it was a close-mouthed smile that gave nothing away. Now he flashed a set of perfectly white teeth that only a few thousand pounds of extreme dentistry or very healthy living could achieve. And then he spoke.

'Hello,' he said

The trace of an accent. A slight smoothing of the vowels and a little constriction in the consonants. Hard to place but not unappealing. Barry's jaw attempted to crunch more ice but there was nothing left but patches of cold. The man extended his hand, offering it for Barry to shake. For a moment Barry hesitated but only because he gripped the tumbler with the hand he needed to use. He placed the tumbler onto the table and leaned forward to meet the strangers welcome.

When their hands met so did their eyes. The stranger's smile broadened causing the edges of his eyes to wrinkle a little. He was a handsome man. Even with what could be considered ridiculous headgear this was something that Barry could see clearly.

He had unblemished skin that looked tanned rather than a product of any particular race. A slim, not too pointed nose supported either side by strong but not prominent cheekbones and which rested above a mouth that produced those perfect teeth and welcoming smile. His eyes were green. The iris's looked like little circles of cracked Emeralds and seemed at odds with his seemingly eastern appearance but somehow enhanced his allure.

'I'm Barry,' he replied.

Utterly caught without guard or the ability to press for answers to the situation Barry decided to wait and see what happened. As was usual.

'It is good to meet you Barry. My name is Ali.' The smile never left his face and as their hands separated Barry noticed how cool, but not cold his skin was. Ali relaxed into the high back of the chair and clasped his hands across his stomach.

'Barry, would you mind if I asked you a few questions?' Barry could not relax as Ali had done and instead sat on the edge of his chair.

'Uh...sure,' he replied, thankful to be given more time to follow what was happening rather than do anything about it.

'Thank you.' Ali replied politely.

'First of all Barry I want to assure you that I am sympathetic with your situation.' Ali paused for a moment to allow that to sink in. 'I want you to know that I understand that your...area of expertise may not be appreciated by many of your people but that *I* can see past their prejudice and unjustified fears.'

Barry sat unmoving but considered this. If this was a dream, disregarding the sheer 'realness' of it all was 'Ali' his own subconscious trying to justify his actions. Barry did not believe that the prejudice and fear people had for what he did was unjustified. In fact he had come to quite the opposite conclusion. He knew was not the smartest of people, that his knowledge of politics, religion...geography was limited at best, he was a bit of a '*softlad.*' But he did know that when people started to praise you for the things you least liked about yourself you had to be cautious.

While Ali had appeared to be so perfect in those first few moments Barry now looked at him differently. His 'ability' was kicking in. He was now starting to read Ali better. What little control he had over this was helped by his mind being calm so now he too relaxed into the chair and because he felt it might help, he smiled a little.

'I am sure that you must be asking yourself 'Where am I?' Ali lifted his hands up and shrugged his shoulders, 'Am I dreaming?' The smile again, large and perfect, meant to be friendly and disarming but Barry now saw something more behind it. There was conceit and arrogance woven into that smile, it was patronising and condescending. It was Mr Singh calling him a 'fucking moron' it was his Dad dismissing the Dreamcatcher he had made at school as 'bits of shit on a string'.

'Yeah, I was thinking that. I think this might be a dream,' Barry said.

Ali nodded, 'Of course, of course, but let me tell you Barry this is not a dream or some moment of madness.'

Ali's expression changed to one of concern.

'You brought yourself out of danger and into a place that I do not have time to explain to you fully but it is a place that I travel frequently and where I can use abilities of my own.'

'I'm sorry, I brought myself to this place?' Barry said, he looked around in confusion.

'Ah, no not to *this* place Barry. This is the Sahara Desert. This is where *I* brought you.'

'I'm sorry I don't follo,.' Barry said with absolute truth.

'Barry first you must understand that your gift, your ability comes from...' Ali paused clearly looking for the right words and Barry was sure he frowned for a moment. Not as someone would when struggling for an answer as someone who didn't like the answer, '...it comes from *how* you are made.'

'I still don't...' Barry tried to say but was quickly cut off.

'Your ability requires an energy Barry. It is fuelled by something that I cannot even begin to explain to you at the moment, but that energy has a source and all that needs to be said is that you were able to escape *into* that source.'

'And that source is here?'

'NO!' Ali snapped.

Barry could see that those few moments of calm and friendly demeanour were a façade that Ali had struggled to maintain. With every minute that passed he could see more of the real creature that hid beneath the skin of this man.

'*I* brought you to here, this is my power at work, my ability,' Ali sat up and the golden threads of the tassel danced a little. 'I saw you being chased by the Paladin, I *knew* that your ability would ensure your safety by bringing you into the Essence.'

Ali's voice began to rise, no longer mellow and slow. His tone was excited and it seemed boastful.

'*I* pulled you from the Essence and into this place. I created this...' he pointed to the Umbrella, 'and this and this,' Ali's hands indicated the table, the chairs, and the water jug.

Barry could have sworn that Ali's emerald iris's fused with his pupils for a moment, becoming solid orbs of an eerie green. Other than this strange thing, that may or not of even happened, Barry could see no change in his appearance but he *could* read more of

115

what made this man tick. Avarice, frustration, anger, violence, loathing, jealousy and lust, to Barry they were all imprinted upon the handsome features like a schematic.

Barry knew how to deal with people like this because he had been ducking under their tempers and whims all his life.

'Wow, that is really impressive,' he said

Ali held his pose for a second his artfully manicured finger pointing at the water jug. His smile returned and shrouded the malice under it.

'Yes, well you too have powers Barry, beyond those you have exercised and this is what I wish to discuss with you.'

Barry felt oddly emboldened. He felt as though he had a measure of this man if not his situation and relaxed a little. He had no doubt that Ali was in turn looking into his face for tell-tale signs of emotion. Now Barry reclined into the chair and managed to give etch a polite smile onto his face. 'I would like to talk about that Ali, very much so,' he said.

'Good, good then let me start with your ability Barry and so that we both understand exactly what we are talking about I shall call it as you do, *Necromancy.*'

Barry offered no flicker of emotion at the word or at least he tried his best not too. He was embarrassed and disgusted with himself concerning this, concerning most things in fact, but this was more than most things.

Ali called it his ability but until recently Barry had thought of it as his trade. Once he had been an odd job man, now he was a Necromancer. Or at least *had been* a Necromancer. Now he wanted nothing to do with it, it had become a curse.

'You can raise the dead Barry, you can usher souls back from… the void to the living world, but do you understand *how* you do this?'

Barry was stumped at this. Despite having performed the ritual over a dozen times he could not honestly say that he had a clue. He often felt a bit like an Encyclopaedia salesman that couldn't read except that this analogy was not really a good one. Not being able to read was the very least of Barry's problems in fact, the truth of the matter the very foundation of all of this trouble was that Barry could read like no one else he had ever heard of.

'I just follow the instructions,' Barry replied.

Ali looked at him with a serious but understanding expression and nodded a little but Barry could see that he was looking at him as though he had just picked his nose and eaten the find.

'The... *instructions* you found in a book Barry, the rituals of Knoph Keh, yes?'

Barry could see no reason to lie and felt that it would be detected if he did however he had said book and not books. Now he could challenge just how much knowledge Ali had about him.

'Yes,' he replied.

'Barry, that book was written in an age when men were *different*, when language had more meaning than it does in your time, how could you know what it said?' Ali asked.

'*He doesn't know,*' Barry thought, '*he doesn't know and he is fishing for answers.*'

Barry responded as earnestly as he could. 'I found the book one day when I was clearing an attic, it was filled with notes and drawings, translations. You know, telling you how to do that kind of stuff.'

'I see,' Ali nodded again and gave Barry the *understanding* and *serious* look, the '*you are a nob-head*' look, 'So tell me please, the Paladin, how did he come to find you out?'

'I'm sorry... the who?' Barry replied.

'Ah... the... *Policeman*, who was hunting you, how did he catch your scent?

Barry recalled that Ali had used the term Paladin just a few moments ago, during his mini-rant. What was a Paladin? He let it lie and decided how best to answer without revealing more than he had too.

'I did a job for a guy, you know a resurrection, it was his son. I was contacted through the Darknet with an offer. Good money, so I went along and did it.'

'*Keep it simple,*' Barry thought as he spoke.

'I have a few rules about how long can pass before it's not safe to do the job and this one was borderline but the guy was really upset and well, in all honesty the money was good.'

A finger of shame traced a line across his forehead and Barry's skin began to glow a little. Ali listened intently but still had the 'you are a nob-head' look, but he clothed it in concern.

'So anyway as ill luck would have it some old lady had a dead cat in her room, don't ask me why, because I haven't a bloody clue, and this copper from the DPI came to investigate.'

Now Ali looked confused, 'dead cat?' he asked, genuinely puzzled.

'Like I said, don't ask me, but I guess the cat got caught up in the ritual, her room was directly above my clients you see, and I suppose the old lady reported it. From then on that massive bastard from the DPI was on my case.'

Ali stroked his chin. The smile had left his face.

'The policeman will be a problem Barry, he will have to be dealt with.' Ali wagged his finger at Barry. 'You will need help to avoid this man and I can assist with this.'

'What do you mean 'dealt with'? He's a copper, he's the law and I don't 'deal with' people. Do I look like someone who *deals* with people?

Ali's patience slipped again. 'He *must* be dealt with Barry he is a threat, a danger to us all. You must open a gate.'

'A gate?' Barry said realsing that he was constantly echoing the last words of Ali's sentences.

Ali ignored him. 'I will be in contact with you shortly. It will be one of my...*friends* that will bring you the required rituals.'

Barry held up a hand to interrupt 'I'm sorry, what? What are you talking about?'

Ali clapped his hands together.

'Unfortunately we have no more time to talk, I must leave.'

He stood and reached into his jacket.

'I will return when able. Use this to return', he placed what looked like a large coin onto the table. 'Meanwhile keep away from the Paladin and look out for my vassal, he will guide you.'

He was gone.

Barry stared at the empty space that Ali occupied just a second ago. One minute there, the next... he scanned the desert, nothing. No one. He stood and exited the shade of the umbrella, instantly the sun beat down upon him as real as anything that he had ever felt. He made his way to the side that Ali had approached from and there in the sand were footsteps leading to the spot.

He followed them out for about ten yards where they abruptly ended. As abruptly as Ali had suddenly disappeared. With no thought of what to do now or where to go he made his way back to the table and poured himself another tumbler of water. Another, smaller and more rounded lump of ice sploshed into the glass.

The coin that Ali had placed onto the table was still there. It was not metal, as he had assumed but wooden and polished. He picked it up and examined each side. On one side, that he would call the 'heads' side was a relief of some sort. It was made up of intricate shapes whose angles seemed to defy any intuitive way of making them fit together. The reverse contained a spiral of glyphs, coiled close together and at the end of the swirl in the dead centre of the coin was a small eye or at least the outline of an eye. There was no lid, or pupil.

He stared at the glyphs intently, and then allowed his eyes to follow the circle they made. Four times around he followed the path they cut into the wood and then finally they became legible to him.

Ali knew that he could do this. It was obvious to Barry that his bluffing may not as been as effective as he might have hoped. Did he know the truth about the book, about the other books?

He returned to his chair and sat, keeping the coin in his hand in case it too suddenly vanished. He needed to study the books. He had promised himself that he wouldn't, that he would sell them to the highest bidder and retire or at least get as far away as possible from the madness that had become commonplace for him.

They scared him. The things that they told him, the things that they could allow him to do, the things that they said existed. And now there was Ali, something else to be scared of? Barry was tired of it, drained by his own fear. He needed to get back and sort things out.

The coin told him what to do. He said the words and was gone, leaving the shaded table and chairs and the jug of water that had two slices of Lime and half melted ice cubes.

Authors comment

Barry's Books was written before Crowley, when I was first putting together ideas for a world in which magic, and forces beyond our dimension, were slowly gaining both power and access. I had begun writing what I hoped would be an epic fantasy tale but had hopelessly overreached my ability at the time, I probably still do. Yet, there were, I thought, some really good characters and concepts in the work I had done before I gave up.

John Creece, of the earlier story with his name is of course the Paladin, and that character was taken almost directly from an idea I had in the fantasy story of a man that is constantly reborn as powerful agent of good for mankind. In Barry's Books, he is the policeman on Barry's trail after his interview with Ms Stack.

As the world has already 'moved on' from what is hinted at in the Crowley series, Barry is a part of a society in which magic is now accepted as a reality and something that has to be closely scrutinized.

This piece is filled with connections of course. It takes place after the events in Creece and has our detective from that short hot on the heels of Barry. Nyarlathotep is referred to in Crowley Vol One (more of that to be seen in Vol Two... one day) and the books are the ones that belonged to the Professor in The Empty God, previous to that you can probably imagine who once owned some of those dreadful tomes.

It's a story that I could never put out as something standalone, except in here, where it is nestled with its cousins. I hope you liked it. Barry has more to do in my future writing.

The Ghost of Claverley Hall

'Ok pal, this is all really great, but what's the deal with the ghost?' The large American man had asked.

He was stood at very fore of the group loosely assembled in front of Martin as he delivered his Visitor Guide Informational Tour. The man's voice was strong, the volume, Martin thought, was needlessly loud for such a small area, especially while other guests were listening quietly, and it was definitely American.

Martin knew the difference between Canadian and American accents, something that often tripped up those who only heard either occasionally. He had spoken with tourists from both countries on many occasions during tours of Claverley Hall and also in the small café situated near to the entrance. He brought to bear no prejudice with this recognition.

American visitors were generally lovely people, especially the youngsters. At least they were, so long as they had come willingly to the Hall and had not been dragged along by teachers or parents, unsure of what to do now in actually in England. These kids, products of a culture almost the same, but not quite, as those of English kids were mostly quite rapt as Martin talked about the history of the Hall. A structure which had been in existence longer than their own country.

But while Claverley Hall had been around for a long time at the end of the day it wasn't as old as or as exciting as The Tower of London. It also wasn't *in* London either. Instead, selfie-seeking tourists of the world had to leave England's capital and travel four hours by coach to take a walk around its nice, but average for a large house, rooms and gardens.

Built in seventeen twenty-eight it had housed barons, dukes and for a short while a prince. Now it was owned by the English Heritage Board, a body who looked after and made available to the public places of historical interest and natural beauty throughout the country. Unfortunately, Martin would be the first to reluctantly agree that Claverley house was a bit dull at best and at worst, very dull.

While it was fairly big, '*but no Chatsworth House,*' he had heard that muttered a few times, and its frontage a quite stunning gothic design, but typical of its day, it didn't really have anything *exceptional* about it. It had its gardens. Nice gardens. But not *great* gardens.

No King or Queen had ever stayed the night. Not even *en route* to somewhere else. No Civil War action had been fought nearby and there had never really been anyone of infamy staying here. Even the Prince had been from Luxembourg. He had stayed for a week and then gone back home, probably bored.

But it did have a ghost.

The ghost of Claverley Hall had never been a big part of its history though, not like some houses who ran entire tours based on grisly or suspicious deaths within or near to their walls. In recent years it had been mentioned only on its Wiki page, which itself was only a couple of paragraphs, and presently in one line on the new information pamphlet.

'Excuse me?' Martin asked politely.

He had been lost in his explanation of how the spinning wheel to his left would be used and who in the household would use it. It was a fantastic piece of beautifully aged and polished wood that was properly equipped with wool and was actually able to be operated. Once, a dear old lady had come along and had sat and used the wheel, producing amazing, colourful lengths of yarn.

'The ghost buddy. What's the story?' the man said impatiently.

Martin took off his glasses and rubbed at them with the bottom of his navy Claverley House Guide tee shirt. Something he did when he needed a little time to catch up with what was going on around him.

'The ghost?' Martin echoed.

The big American lifted up a Claverley Hall pamphlet, it seemed tiny in his large chubby hands. He was easily six-feet tall and carried a huge amount of weight. His face, his hands, his legs and his gut all smacked of years of self-gratification and laziness.

'*Oh my,*' thought Martin, '*that is a very well fed guy.*'

Whenever he saw guests this size he couldn't help but think of the Fatties from his 2000AD comic books. Enormous people, so obese they required wheels under their bellies to support them and enable them to get around. Martin had always wanted to be

Judge Dredd when he was a child, but he became a tour guide because that's where GCSEs in History and English took you if you didn't also get Maths.

The large man began to read from the pamphlet.

'Claverley Hall is a remarkably well kept Gothic style building erected in the seventeen hundreds. It has been home to many of England's noble family's, has a working farm on the grounds *and its very own ghost*,' He looked up to Martin from the pamphlet with demanding eyes.

'Oh right, of course,' Martin said, now back on track, *'terrific,'* he thought.

He licked his lips and tried his best to smile. It was a pain being interrupted during his memorised script as he would then have to remember where he had got to. If he couldn't, he would have to go over it all again and he knew that it would be tedious for the guests.

'Well, there's not really much to tell, he said, and as he did so the Americans face fell.

'What? Whaddya mean not much to tell. If you gotta ghost you must have a ghost story.'

The big man turned and lifted his hands, seeking support from the other onlookers. His expression said quite clearly, 'can you believe this guy?'

Martin thought quickly. *Mr Fat Bastard* was clearly going to be a problem if he was allowed to keep talking. Reluctantly Martin pulled up his memory of the tale concerning the ghost. The problem was there really *wasn't* much to tell.

'Well Sir,' Martin began, *'you massive fat bastard,'* he thought, 'The ghost is believed to be that of a young lady who worked at the hall in a domestic capacity.'

'What, like a cleaner or something?' Fat Bastard said.

'Uh…yes, a little,' Martin replied, 'domestics would attend to the day to day activity required of such a large house as this.'

'They get minimum wage, huh?' The American laughed loudly at this clearly believing he had said something funny. Martin ignored this and replied as factually as he could.

'Well, not as we would know it but yes they would have been paid a very small amount for their labours.'

'Yeah,' Fat Bastard replied, 'ain't that just typical of the aristocrats.'

123

Once again he turned to the group, nodding with the implicit understanding that they should nod also. To Martins dismay a few of them did. Probably cowed by this huge, loud man. He hurried on.

'Well this particular lady unfortunately was very ill, probably something that these days would have been spotted and possibly cured, but back then, it was the early eighteen hundreds, medicine was still in its infancy and so…'

'Are you going to tell me that this chick died of natural causes?' Fat Bastard boomed.

Martin blinked, 'Well… yes, she passed away due to her illness.'

'Well Jeez, what kind of ghost story is *that?*' Fat Bastard asked with no small amount of disapproval.

A stick thin woman beside him piped up, 'Yeah, holy cow… is that it *Martin*, cos that's kinda lame.'

Martin was surprised that he hadn't noticed her, she was stood right up against Fat Bastard. She was so slightly built that she looked as though she also might be ill, an eating disorder perhaps.

'*Lord knows watching Fat Bastard eat probably puts her off mealtimes,*' he thought.

She had clearly read his name badge and he didn't like the way she drawled *Martin* out, as though she were addressing an imbecile. Side by side he thought that they looked like the number ten. He assumed that this must be *Mrs Bastard.*

'Natural causes, yes. She was working right here, spinning yarn for the seamstress of the house when her illness overcame her and she collapsed.'

Martin pointed to the wheel. He had never really given it much thought, that a person, a young girl no less, had died at the very spot where he would drone on about servants, textiles and local crafts. He had certainly not given the story of the ghost of the young girl any consideration. And why would he? No one ever reported strange sounds, moving furniture or cold spots, at least not since the very early days.

He knew that people had come in the past, especially during the Victorian era and early nineteen hundreds. There was a mad craze for the paranormal back then. Even Sir Arthur Conan Doyle had come to look into it, Madame Blavatsky and Aleister Crowley were also said to have been here. But apparently they had concluded that there was nothing. Which made sense to Martin because there was no such thing as ghosts.

'Well, how sad,' Fat Bastard said unimpressed.

Martin pressed on, not prepared to let the American slow him down. 'Afterwards there were stories, people, other workers claimed that they saw the girl, or her image at least. She was said to look lost, she wandered the halls.'

'She scare anyone, she *kill* anyone?' Mrs Bastard asked.

'Gosh no,' Martin said, 'I believe that the sightings didn't last very long and nothings been heard of her since.'

He looked at the rest of the group for the first time since being interrupted and realised that they were getting as bored of this as he was of the annoying American.

'There have been more ghost hunters here than ghosts it seems,' Martin issued a small and nervous laugh. He hoped that they would laugh a little with him and it would signify the end of this detour from the script.

'*Gahhd,* you were right Bernie, this place really sucks,' Mrs Bastard said, more to Martin than to her husband.

'Bernie,' Martin thought, '*Bernie the Bastard.*'

'I told ya. Didn't I say? Bernie the Bastard said, and he turned to his captive audience once again.

'Man, you want some proper ghost stories you came to the U S of A. We got shit that'll make yah hair stand up.' He laughed. Not a friendly laugh. It was the laugh of a schoolyard bully who has just pushed you to the floor and pointed out to everyone how weak and girly you are.

Martin offered another laugh by way of disingenuous agreement. As the English do. Thanking you for your input while silently plotting your absolute and total downfall.

He decided to skip the rest of the Spinning Wheel talk and head over to the kitchen. Of which he had no doubt Bernie the Bastard would have some criticism.

'Lovely, lovely,' he said. 'Well folks let's move on, lots more to see in Claverley Hall and don't forget that its lunchtime at twelve thirty in the *Claverley Olde Worlde Restaurant.*'

Martin hated the name of what was actually a very small café and one that served Costa Coffee, which he was certain didn't count as *Olde Worlde.*

He led the guests out of the room and they shuffled along behind him.

***

Mary had watched and listened to Martin. As she did almost every day. She liked him. He was funny, in a timid way. He enjoyed talking about the house, about its history. He was always very attentive to the children and to the older people who struggled to hear him occasionally, for although he loved to tell the tales of Claverley he wasn't loud. Unlike the large man. The large man had been rude.

She knew that she had been in the house for a long, long time. Martin repeated the dates all the time and although she could do her numbers quite well she could not make the time he was talking about connect in any way with her sense of actually being there. For her, when the days passed, when the house was closed for the evening and opened in the morning they were simply part of the *same* day. Open and closed meant nothing, seconds, minutes, hours, years meant *nothing*.

Mary knew what she was. She was lucky, she understood that. She had been *told*. The man had come along and explained it all to her, one of the many people who had visited the Hall because she was there. She liked him. The others who had come to try and speak to her, they were focused, scary people. They knocked on the walls and lifted the furniture, they scattered powders about place and used devices to try and *capture her*.

They hadn't come for a long time now, as little as time meant she knew that it had been a while since the folks who wanted to see her given up.

But the nice man, when he had come along he had spoken to her regardless of her staying quiet. She didn't think he could see her, but then he didn't even try. Mary knew was a very naughty fellow, he couldn't hide his mischievous side from her. She also knew that he could be sly, foxy and a ladies man too, people couldn't hide themselves from her because they unwittingly carried their nature about them in the beautiful radiance the living gave off.

And even as he sat and talked with her, a spirit he couldn't see or hear, and surely he couldn't know for sure was listening, he was still roguish and flirted. He was funny and charming and told wonderful stories. His name was Aleister.

At seventeen she was not unaccustomed to the charming ways of men but this gentlemen, for she could tell he was a real gentleman, had a devilish allurement about him. She couldn't help but listen to him as he sat, alone in the house. He had insisted that all other occupants leave him be for a while.

He had told her that she was currently stuck in the house. That it was a place where a special kind of energy was very strong. Because of this it was very difficult for young people, who not had enough time to absorb the special energy from the world around them and who had sadly passed on, to move away and onwards with their journey.

He said that while she might feel the need to be sad or perhaps angry and confused, she should refrain. She should store the energy, which would slowly be absorbed by her spirit, so that one day she would be strong enough to break away from the attraction of the house.

'Conserve your energy child. Do not strike out unless it is to save your spirit from those who would force you to a place that you will not want to go,' he said.

He had stroked the top of the Spinning Wheel lightly, with a father's tenderness.

'You are in a lovely house. Look after it and it will look after you I'm sure,' and with that he kissed the tips of his fingers and gently placed them upon the spindle.

She had never forgotten that strange and wonderful man and she had always remained hidden as he had advised. Trying only to watch, only to listen.

Lately, she had begun to feel that the energy the gentlemen had said would come to her had grown, so steadily and slowly that it was like watching the big hand of the grandfather clock in the long room move. But she had not always been able to stay quite still.

The big man had been terrible to Martin. Had upset him a little. She could feel his emotions as he stood by her spinning wheel and so, from it, she extended her arm, a truly ghostly reach. The, silvery stream of her energy, invisible to most, drifted through the house, down stairs and along corridors. It reached the dining room, where the visitors to her lovely house sat and ate. Most of them talked about the wonderful rooms and paintings, the opulent beds and the children were excited about the petting zoo and farm animals that lay beyond the grounds.

The fat man and his shrewish wife had seated themselves next to Martin. They moaned at him, and chided his position. They were mean and thoughtless and Mary would not allow it any longer. She cared for this house, her home for so long, and she loved the people who took care of it, who explained its history to others so that they might come to love it also.

Her translucent hand glided forward, invisible to all except dogs who occasionally came in with sightless owners. She reached in to the ample chest of the big man and gently caressed the overworked heart at the centre of it. She could almost feel the heat of this organ as it worked furiously, and yet, like poor Martin, was considered without respect from the mind that operated it.

She allowed a little of the energy she had been conserving all this time to pass through her. Only a little though. The mischievous gentleman had told her not to draw attention to herself or the house.

'*If you must act, make it nothing too naughty my lady,*' he had said.

And so she only gave him the lightest of contacts. The touch of a ghost.

Bernie suddenly felt his chest tighten. He had been devouring a large bun, filled with chicken and salad. He had complained that it was tiny, 'Jeez, nearly eight bucks U.S for that little thing.' Now the chicken pieces that slid down his throat felt like they were the size of cinder blocks.

He coughed. A couple of pieces flew out of his mouth and landed on the table.

'Bernie! For Pete's sake, use a tissue!' His wife had scowled out from thin ruby red lips.

Bernie brought both his hands to his chest as though he was trying to grip his heart through his ribs.

'Gnnnnnghnnnn.' He said.

'Sir, are you OK?' Martin asked. All loathing cast aside as his natural sense of compassion came to the fore.

Bernie looked at him with a mix of fear and anger. '*Why was the little prick sat there staring? Couldn't he see he was having a heart atta…*'

His legs stiffened and pushed the vast bulk of his body backwards. The chair tipped and he went crashing onto the floor, still clutching his chest.

'Ambulance!' Martin shouted. He's having some kind of seizure!'

Mrs Bastard screamed in his ear. A piercing, shrill sound that made Martin flinch.

He dropped to his knees next to Bernie the Bastard and loosened his shirt collar. He had been trained for this kind of thing. He knew what to do. He would do his very best to make sure that this overweight, self-indulgent, sweaty, ignorant loudmouth lived.

And that is why Mary liked Martin. He was good at heart. It was worth a few more decades in the house to look after him. She smiled and retreated her ethereal hand to the spinning wheel and for old time's sake made it turn, just a little.

TWO DOORS UP

Aiden would have bet his life that the Prendevilles, just two doors up from his Dad's house, were Vampires. The evidence was clear to him, irrefutable and there was lots of it.

How he could have been so wrong continued to remain a mystery to him.

The press had dubbed him 'The Smiling Slasher,' which Aiden felt was very misleading. There had been no slashing at all. In fact the only point at which he had used a knife on the Prendevilles was to decapitate them, and that had been more of a sawing motion. You certainly couldn't call it slashing.

In truth it had been surprisingly difficult to remove their heads with the knife. Even the children had been a bother. Mr Prendeville had been so tough to get through that Aiden had actually considered going back to his house to fetch Dad's handsaw. But time was against him.

His goal had been to start at 2am and be finished by no later than 3. There was no school as it was the weekend but he had arranged to go swimming with his friends in the morning. Unfortunately, it was closer to 5am when Mrs Prendeville's spine finally gave up and he has able to cut through the last bit of skin and gristle. And you *still* couldn't call it 'slashing' and of course the job wasn't completely done at that point.

He had begun his work after breaching the lairs defences via a loose back window, and by creeping into the bedroom and striking Mr Prendeville solidly across the temple with Dad's ball-pein hammer he achieved complete surprise. There had been a dull thud and other than his head being pushed a little deeper into the pillow there was no sign of Mr P reacting to the blow.

Mrs Prendeville didn't stir at all and just to be sure that Mr P wasn't going to leap up and tear his throat out, he had seen enough Wes Craven movies not to fall for that old trick,

Aiden swung again. This time there was a satisfying *crack*. By the faint light cast through the curtains he saw Mr P's eye bulge out a little under the eyelid. He made his way around the bed to Mrs P who still slept soundly.

For a moment a little confusion crept into his thoughts, as he raised the hammer high above his head. A question floated by, nudging at him, upsetting his concentration.

Why did the Prendevilles sleep at night?

Fortunately, his wits were about him and he remembered. This was not a family of ordinary vampires. He was well aware that there are all kinds of different types, different breeds with special powers. These were Daywalkers!

He brought the hammer down.

Using a tent spike he staked each of the bodies. Aiden was very pleased that his delivery of the weapon had been near perfect. He had felt for the breastbone, and just to the right targeted the point just two fingers width away from there. Two hard and accurate strikes had plunged the peg into deep into each chest leaving only a couple inches of it protruding.

All that remained was to turn the Nosferatu to ashes. As it was much later than he had anticipated Aiden contemplated simply opening the curtains in each room and letting the sunlight do its work. Then he recalled that the Prendevilles had some sort of resistance to this, them being Daywalkers and all that.

They often left the house during the day. Both kids went to the junior school near to where his gran lived. Mr P masqueraded as an accountant. He wasn't sure what Mrs Prendeville did to disguise her real nature but Aiden didn't think it mattered now, what was important was that the street was safe.

He decided that it was best to stick with the original plan and set the house alight, but not before taking a photo. Beaming with pride, he stretched out his arm and pointed the iPhone toward his face. With the bloody corpses of the

Prendeville children just visible behind him he pressed the button.

He updated his Facebook status with the picture and a comment.

'Got em folks!'

He had been relieved when the court had declared that he was not insane (as his idiot defence lawyer had tried to claim).

'As such you will feel the full force of the law,' the Judge had said in his summation.

Aiden had liked the Judge; he seemed to know what he was doing. The Judge clearly understood that he had just been mistaken, but obviously people had been hurt so Aiden would have to go to prison for a bit.

Prison was fine. Aiden had a great cellmate named Jasper who liked to masturbate him, which was pretty cool. The other inmates gave him a wide birth. Even the scary looking ones kept their distance, which Aiden thought was odd. He always tried to be friendly.

There was one problem though. Something Aiden had realised, and that obviously no one else had noticed. The lads two cells up from his were quite clearly Zombies. Fortunately, Aiden knew exactly how to handle that.

Afterword

2015 was a big year for me. I both wrote and released Crowley, all four parts within eight months, and completed and published my novel Winter Falls in the same period. In between this I produced the stories you have just read with the exception of The Whitby Horror and Two Doors Up which I wrote in 2014. It was a hell of a time.

Being self-published I had very little pressure and manageable, low expectations, and I was lucky I had the drive to get them all done. I was pushed on by a remarkable people and kept on course by authors who had been published professionally and who also held no fear of pointing out my failings. It was a good mix.

As I write this I have a new novel underway and a Volume Two of the Crowley series mapped out. I've got a Sci-fi series I'm working on and with any luck I'll be able to work on another novel later in the year, this one unconnected with the 'Aether' series. I also have a hard drive filled with half-finished works that will need some attention and the obligatory audiobook to produce.

I hope you will stick around and see what comes next. Should be fun.

Eddie Skelson May 2016